BOUNTY HUNTER DOWN UNDER

S.C. STOKES

PRESCIENT PUBLISHING

Copyright © 2022 by Prescient Publishing & S.C. Stokes

All rights reserved.

No portion of this book may be reproduced in any form without written permission from the publisher or author, except as permitted by U.S. copyright law.

For my mother Jenny, she shared her love of reading with me and it changed my world.

Contents

A Note From The Author	VII
1. Chapter 1	1
2. Chapter 2	11
3. Chapter 3	20
4. Chapter 4	28
5. Chapter 5	40
6. Chapter 6	52
7. Chapter 7	64
8. Chapter 8	77
9. Chapter 9	89
10. Chapter 10	98
11. Chapter 11	108
12. Chapter 12	123
13. Chapter 13	133
14. Chapter 14	148
15. Chapter 15	162

16. Chapter 16	172
17. Chapter 17	182
18. Chapter 18	191
Thank You For Being Here	200
Glossary Of Aussie Slang	202
Have You Read A Date With Death?	205
About the Author	207
Also By S.C. Stokes	208

A Note From The Author

Welcome to *Bounty Hunter Down Under*. I'm delighted to have you here. Before we dive in, I wanted to take a quick moment to mention the linguistic choices in the novel.

Naturally it's set here in Australia, so you'll find a few classic Aussie terms in here. For fun I've included a glossary at the end. Hand on my heart, the definitions are straight out of the Oxford dictionary.

That said, the book is written in US English, with the singular exception of the word mum when used in dialogue.

Are you ready? Enter the magical midlife crisis of Nora Byrne.

I'll see you on the other side.

S.C. Stokes

Chapter 1

When the gods that give out magical talent got to me, they were either asleep or three sheets to the wind.

Perhaps they just have a cruel sense of humor. While there were witches and wizards with enough power to level a city block, I could do little more than chill a drink.

Winter's Touch, they called it.

I was about as dangerous as a refrigerator in good working order.

In spite of my shortcomings, here I was, alone, and facing down four of the most dangerous creatures known to man. Just me and my fridge fingers.

The door handle felt cool to the touch, or perhaps that was just me. Did I actually have to brave the chaos within?

From the racket, it sounded like all hell was breaking loose in there, but I had no choice. I took a deep breath and embraced my fate.

I let out the breath and accepted my fate. This was my life now.

Twisting the handle, I pushed open the door. My ears were assailed by what had to be one hundred decibels of Taylor Swift's latest hit blaring so loudly I was stunned the window was still in its frame. Four fourteen-year-old girls danced around the room, arms flailing like drunken windmills, screaming the lyrics along with their favorite star.

My daughter and one of her friends jumped up onto the bed, its frame creaking under the abuse.

None of them seemed to even notice my entry.

"Shay!" I shouted, trying to be heard over the ruckus. It was like trying to scream into a cyclone.

When none of them responded, I strode across the room and turned off the speakers.

The dancing came to an abrupt halt.

"Hey Mum, what did you do that for?" my daughter called from her place at the edge of the bed.

She looked up at me with big brown eyes. Her short mousy brown hair looked like it hadn't been brushed yet this morning. With the dancing, I'm not sure it would have made much difference. Neither Shay nor her three slumber party guests looked like they were ready to tackle the day. Neither did they show any signs of slowing down.

Part of me was quite pleased that I was heading in to work. It was going to be a hell of a lot quieter there than around here.

Did that make me a bad mom?

I took two steps to the edge of the bed, grabbed her face in my palms, and kissed her forehead.

"Mum, everyone is watching," she said through gritted teeth.

"I'm off to work. Granny will be here any minute. Behave yourself and watch out for your brother."

"Do I have to?" Her syllables grew longer with every word as I headed for the door.

"Only if you ever want to have another sleepover," I replied. "And turn it down a little. You'll all go deaf."

I closed the door behind me, and it was all of a second before the music fired up again, marginally quieter than before.

"I'll take that as a yes," I told myself.

As I raced down the stairs, my calf muscles burned and my breath quickened at the exertion. I really needed to take better care of myself, but right now I was flat out trying to take care of my kids. I just never seemed to have any time left for me. The girls had kept me up half the night and the lack of sleep was taking a toll. Not a good sign with the day only just beginning.

I couldn't party like I used to. Not that I was ever a big party goer, but there was a time when I could read all night and roll out the door on an hour or two of sleep none the worse for wear.

Granted, that was when I was eighteen, not forty-two, so I figured that was just a part of getting older.

A part that could go right to hell, and take my ex-husband, Judas, with it.

That wasn't his name of course, but after he'd ditched me for a legal secretary a little more than half my age, it felt appropriate.

I rummaged about in the bowl on our dining table and found my keys and my phone. Tossing them both in my handbag, I headed for the fridge. There really wasn't time to fix anything at home, but I could always snack on something on the way in. I walked to work most days. After all, the office wasn't far. I tried to tell myself it was for the exercise, but the reality was petrol was optional; paying our rent was not. Doing them on one paycheck seemed a little harder every week.

My stomach rumbled as I opened the fridge. There was a plate of choc-chip muffins I'd prepared for the kids for morning tea. My eyes played over the chocolate buttons I'd pressed into the batter and my mouth watered.

Can you really afford one of those? my inner critic whispered. She could be a real witch sometimes. I garnered what self-control I could muster, ignored the muffins, and pulled a small Greek yogurt off the shelf. Adding a spoon from the kitchen drawer, I tossed them both in my bag.

I'd have chosen something more substantial but summer with all the Christmas and New Year feasting had done a real number on my waist, and I was determined to stay in these pants come hell or high water. So, yogurt would have to do. No fat, no flavor; mmm, just how I liked it. Not.

Looking up, I found my twelve-year-old son, Conor, sitting at the kitchen counter, a half-eaten bowl of Weet-Bix pushed to one side and his sketch pad open in front of him.

Unlike his sister, he was fair-skinned with blond hair and blue eyes.

He scribbled on the pad, oblivious to my presence, largely on account of the noise-canceling headphones he usually saved for being outdoors.

Crowds, noisy places, and background racket in general didn't agree with him.

Unlike most people, he couldn't just tune out background conversations and the chatter of suburbia. The headphones made life a little less hectic. With his sister upstairs waging World War Swift, I understood their presence. We weren't a loud family, not after his father moved out anyway, but today was an exception. School holidays were coming to an end, so I'd let Shay have her friends stay over.

Glancing down at my watch, I noted the time. If my mother wasn't here soon, I was going to be late for work.

I considered calling her, but like Gandalf, Cara Byrne arrived precisely when she meant to. The fact that was often a good twenty minutes after you expected her was something I'd gotten used to during my life.

Reaching into my bag, I pulled out the yogurt and peeled off the lid. I licked the lid and muffled a sigh. It tasted like disappointment.

Ignoring the blandness of my breakfast, I made my way over to where Conor sat and bent down beside him, examining his work. He had a steady hand and an incredible imagination. Scrawled over the A3 piece of paper was a charcoal black castle resting on a frosty mountain peak. The castle seemed to stand out from the page and was meticulously detailed, from the chains lowering the drawbridge, to a winged creature soaring through the air high above it. If I had to guess, I'd say it was from one of his video games. Conor loved those things, but I worried he spent too much time on them and not enough in the real world.

It took him a few moments to realize I was there. I hadn't wanted to startle him.

He slid the headphones down his neck, wincing at the chaos upstairs.

Looking up at me, he managed a quiet, "Hi, Mum."

He didn't say a lot, but somehow, he always managed to fit a lot of feeling into every word. And the little smile he gave me warmed my heart.

"Hey little guy, what are you drawing?"

He looked down at his paper and shrugged. "Just something I saw."

Picking up his pencil, he continued shading.

"It's very good," I replied.

I meant it, and I thought it was important for him to hear. Growing up, praise in my family had been hard won. I had never known my dad, and my mom was something of a hard ass, the result of her having to play Dad as well as Mom.

I wanted to make sure my kids didn't grow up with the same lack of confidence I had been blessed with.

Not that Conor needed hollow praise; the picture was impressive. I was going to have to find him an outlet to help cultivate his talents. Perhaps there was an art class in the community somewhere. It might help him make a friend, too.

"Well, buddy, Mum has to head into work shortly. Granny's going to look after you and your sister. Try to be good for her, okay?"

Conor nodded. When it came to babysitting him, my mother wouldn't have to work too hard. Watching the four escape artists upstairs, was a whole different matter. I figured the two kind of balanced each other out. Or at least repaid her for some of the mischief she'd caused me over the years.

The front door swung open without a knock, revealing my mother, Cara, a gray-haired woman in her sixties.

"Nora." Her voice boomed as she competed with Taylor Swift. "An unlocked door. You might as well send the Sidhe an engraved invitation."

That was my mother for you. More concerned about the Fae than the drug dealer down the street.

"I was expecting you," I called back. "Besides, the Sidhe aren't going to want to compete with all that."

I pointed upstairs, more to humor my mother than anything else. She had drummed into me that the supernatural world existed beyond the borders of our own, but I'd never seen a Sidhe outside of a book of fairy tales, and if it wasn't for Mom always harping on about them I doubt I'd give them a second thought.

The Otherworld didn't bother with us, and that was how I liked it. Or at least, so I thought.

"What in all the hells is that racket?" Mother asked.

"Your granddaughter is hosting a slumber party," I said with a smile. Bending down, I kissed Conor on the forehead. "Be good for your grandmother, would you?"

My mother strode across the room and gave him a big bear hug.

"Oh, we'll be good all right, won't we?" She bent down and gave him a conspiratorial wink.

Conor giggled, a sound that made my soul soar. His boyish laugh seemed to incite pure joy in those around him. Conor and my mother got along spectacularly, which was a miracle in and of itself. My mother hardly got along with anyone. She was of old Irish stock, and stubbornness ran like concrete through her veins.

Mine too for that matter, or so Judas had always told me.

"Thanks for taking care of them, Mum. I should be back just after five."

I gave her a hug, which was akin to trying to embrace a stout brick pillar, and headed for the door.

"That's interesting," my mother whispered as she bent over the sketchpad. "Now where did you see that?"

I smiled as I pulled the door closed behind me. Bouncing down the front steps, I set off across the lawn. A sharp bark made me jump.

There waiting at the fence was Bran. The old shaggy Irish wolfhound was a monstrous animal with an equally large heart. We had found him abandoned in a park not long after Conor had been born; he'd been weather beaten with thick matted fur. I had been amazed he'd managed to survive the heat here. He looked every part the lost stray, and while Judas had been adamant we take him to the pound, Shay wasn't having a bar of it. So, home he'd come with us, and he'd been our loyal guardian ever since.

I hurried to the fence, reached over it, and ran my hands through the thick gray fur on his neck.

How he managed to keep it that thick while living in this climate was beyond me. Beenleigh, Australia, located half an hour from the Gold Coast and about twenty minutes from the surface of the sun. It was a miracle to me that he didn't overheat. We'd tried to cut his fur once, but he'd made it clear that it was there to stay. We let him have his way and did what we could to help him stay cool, a struggle considering he refused to spend any meaningful amount of time indoors.

"I'd love to take you for a walk, big guy, but I've gotta head in to work. These bills won't pay themselves and after Judas left, that's a lot harder than it used to be."

Bran panted, his big pink doggy tongue dangling out of his open jaws.

I ran my hand over him, noting the heat rising from his coat. I glanced up and down the street, but couldn't see anyone. Closing my eyes, I gathered what power I could muster and channeled it until icy cool mist poured from my open palm.

Bran brushed up against my hand, using it to cool himself down. It was a neat trick, one of the only ones I knew. When it had first happened to me, I was convinced I was a witch. At least, until my mom had had me tested.

A minor magical talent, the examiner had said. An innate talent suited only for simple manipulations of the arcane, but nothing more. I'd played with it as a teenager, but it was little more than a novelty.

These sorts of talents tended to run in the family, but I'd never seen my mother do anything like it. When I'd pressed her about it, all she'd been willing to say was that it was something I must have inherited from my father. Given he wasn't in the picture, that was about as far as the conversation had gone. According to Ma, Dad had been a workaholic, and she'd left him in Ireland to spare herself the misery of his company. Judas and my father seemed to have a few things in common.

Us Byrne women knew how to pick them.

Fridge hands, that was my talent. There was no one coming to whisk me off to an academy filled with gifted youngsters and whimsical teachers. No, a minor magical talent was merely good for party tricks. At least it came in handy; I hadn't had to drink a lukewarm beverage in years. Unfortunately, drink chilling as an occupation had stiff competition. So, I'd had to find a real job.

Confucius said, 'choose a job you love, and you'll never have to work a day in your life.' I had taken that to heart and chosen something that made me happy. There certainly wasn't big money in being a librarian, but I could walk there every day with a smile on my face.

"I'll take you out for a stroll tonight, I promise," I replied, ruffling the fur behind Bran's ears.

I stepped away from the fence and headed for the footpath, narrowly avoiding a small pile of dog poo in the middle of my lawn. It wasn't Bran's; he would never leave it in the middle of the yard like a barbarian. This was one of my neighbor's dogs, and if I was ever up early enough to catch them in their morning ritual, I was going to be sure to give them a piece of my mind.

Or my fridge hands. Just kidding; using my powers on a normal was certain to get me into strife.

Except confrontation wasn't my way. I was far more likely to freeze the poo and leave it in their car's exhaust pipe, or jam it into their letterbox. I let my imagination run wild with all the things I might do, as I made my way to work.

Glancing at my watch again, I picked up the pace. I was going to be late. Maybe only ten or fifteen minutes but if Karen caught me, she was certainly going to let me know about it.

Karen was the only bad thing about work. She was born without empathy and had a personality that was as exciting as a cheese grater and just as personable. Luckily, she spent most of her time in her office, leaving me to work in peace.

Fortunately, I lived close to work. I had picked the cheap rental for that very reason. With Judas gone, I needed to tighten the belt buckle. Rent here in this part of town was affordable, though barely, and we were walking distance to school and work.

It wasn't perfect—in fact, the neighborhood was a hot mess—but we made do.

Because that was what you did when your life came apart at the seams. You grabbed both edges and held on for dear life. That and hope whatever gods of karma were watching came out of retirement and got to work on your ex as soon as possible. I tried not to be bitter, but if his new girlfriend happened to trip over her ridiculous heels and twist her ankle, I'd take that as a bonus.

I walked along the footpath, through Beenleigh, a patch of suburbia located halfway between the world-famous Gold Coast and the state capital, Brisbane. It was perhaps best known for its rum distillery, famous meat pie shop, Yatala Pies, and a train station that opened a century ago. What had started as a tired little town had grown into a suburban sprawl clustered around the town center. We had our own post office, a local magistrates court, a police station, and one of my favorite places in the world: the library.

Which also happened to be where I worked.

As the library came into view, I tossed the yogurt container into a trash can beside the footpath, stashed the spoon in my bag, and picked up the pace.

Two police cars sat in the no-parking bay out front, their red and blue lights flashing angrily.

My heart kicked up. Why would the police be here? Outside the library?

I raced across the grassy lawn, disturbing a ring of wild mushrooms growing there. Two of the bulbous fungi went flying and I could hear my mother's voice in my head, warning me of the Fae and their portals to the Otherworld.

Pushing her words from my mind, I dipped my head in respect as I passed the Anzac war memorial and bounded up the library stairs, taking them two at a time.

Reaching the top, I discovered the library's large sliding glass doors, usually the welcoming portals to my favorite sanctuary, had been completely obliterated.

There was glass everywhere. Strangely, it seemed scattered over the tiles outside the library, like something had burst through them in a hurry to leave.

What on earth had happened here?

Chapter 2

I made my way gingerly through the sea of ruined doors and came face-to-face with a police officer. Well, face to chest. He was a few inches over six feet tall and I had to raise my eyes just to meet his gaze. He held out a hand to stop me as I approached.

"Sorry, ma'am, library is shut today."

"It's Nora, not ma'am, please. That makes me feel even older, and I don't know about you, but I don't need any more of that in my life."

That brought a sheepish grin to his face. "I hear you, but the library is closed to guests, Nora."

"Good thing I'm not a guest, then," I replied. "I work here, and I really need to get inside. I'm running late and would rather my boss found me in there, than out here, if you know what I mean."

"Your boss wouldn't happen to be Karen, would it?" He said it the same way you'd talk about a sleeping dingo: quietly, so it didn't wake up and bite you in the ass.

"Got it in one," I replied, peering through the doors to see if I could spot her.

"Best of luck to you," the officer replied, taking half a step back out of the way. "Seems like everyone is tidying up. We're just about done here."

As I passed him, my gaze returned to the broken doors. "Any idea what happened?"

It looked like something the size of a truck had exited the library without opening the doors first. But the handrails running down the center of the stairs were intact, and anything that large would have broken the railing to pieces.

"We're still trying to work that out," the officer replied. "Unfortunately, the security cameras malfunctioned. Didn't catch anything. Same with the ones over the road."

I followed his finger to the building across the street. It was a concrete construction that housed one of the larger banks in town.

"Who'd want to rob a library when there's a bank right across the road?" I asked.

The officer shrugged. "If you work that one out, be sure to let us know. Not like there was any cash here, right? Doesn't seem like they did anything other than trash the place. Current theory is a bundle of bored teenagers broke in and vandalized the place for something to do."

I let out a sigh. "Story of my life, teenagers making messes for me to clean up."

"You've got kids, then?" the officer asked.

"Yep, two of them. Fourteen and twelve. They can be trying, but neither of them would ever do anything like this."

"Mine, either," he replied. "Three and seven. They're angels when they're sleeping."

I laughed. "Just wait until they're teenagers."

"Nora, stop flirting with the officer and get in here," Karen called from the library. "We've got work to do."

I looked at the officer and rolled my eyes. "Duty calls."

Karen was able to suck the joy out of the world with a single sentence. It was a talent.

Treading carefully, I made my way into the library to find Karen waiting, her hands on her hips and a scowl on her lips.

"This is the second time this week you've been late," she said.

Her silver-gray hair was pulled back into a tight bun that only made the throbbing vein on her temple stand out more.

"I was waiting for the sitter. It's the school holidays. I couldn't leave the kids at home alone."

Karen held up a hand. "Always an excuse, Nora. You need to get yourself together. If it keeps happening, I'll be issuing a formal warning."

There were people in this world who took whatever little bit of power they had and exercised it to make others miserable. Such creatures learned their trade from Karen. If I didn't need this job so badly, I'd have considered trying to answer one of life's great questions: would Karen fit in the book return chute? There was really only one way to find out.

Conflict and I really didn't agree though. I swallowed my pride, nodded, and found myself muttering, "It won't happen again."

"See that it doesn't," Karen said. "Now go make yourself useful tidying up."

"Anywhere in particular you'd like me to start?" I asked, trying not to vomit as I sought my way back into her good graces. I really couldn't afford to be fired.

Karen swept her hand through the air. "The place is trashed. Most of the shelves have been righted. Let's get the books re-shelved. We have our work cut out for us, if we hope to reopen anytime soon."

My heart skipped a beat. What did she mean reopen anytime soon? I was only a casual employee. I needed my shifts just to make rent.

I couldn't afford to miss a day, so I looked for somewhere to start.

"Sure thing, Karen," I said before leaving her in the foyer. I wanted to be anywhere other than where she was. Seeing as she had given me carte blanche to pick my punishment, I headed deeper into the library.

I found Sally, my partner in crime, in the cubicles cleaning out our workstations. She was wearing a pair of hipster jeans that made me envy her waistline. Her dyed blond hair was pulled back into a ponytail, and her silver glasses rested low on her nose.

The cubicles looked like what happened when a hurricane hit an office supply store. Paper and personal effects were scattered everywhere. I took one look at my desk and wished I hadn't.

"Little beggars." I grimaced as I noticed my favorite coffee cup in several pieces on the floor. It was a custom painted mug that had been intricately styled with bookshelves around the face. Bending down, I picked up the handle; it still had half a bookshelf attached to it.

This day kept getting better and better.

"Morning, Nora," Sally said without looking up from the mountain of papers she was gathering together. Sally Johnson had been working here almost as long as I had, and shared my love of reading. There was no way of telling how many hours we'd whiled away talking about our favorite reads. I tended to enjoy losing myself in fantasy worlds. Sally favored romance and the steamier it got, the more she liked it.

I enjoyed a good romance myself, but with everything going on in my own life, I wasn't much in the mood for reading about what my hormones reminded me I was missing out on.

"Little vandals trashed everything," Sally said with a pained sigh. "Sorry about your cup."

The contents of our cubicles had been dumped on the floor. It was going to take hours to sort through everything. The mug was just the icing on the cake. I didn't keep many personal things in the office, but they'd managed to find it anyway. "It happens," I replied. "I think I'd rather be somewhere else right now. I'm going to head into the shelves and start picking up books. You got things here?"

Sally nodded. "I don't know about got, but I'll keep at it. I'll join you out there when I'm done."

I glanced at my cubicle and stopped. The little corkboard I kept there was empty. Normally there were a handful of pictures of Shay and Conor pinned to it. Now there was nothing but thumbtacks.

"Hey Sally, you haven't found my pictures anywhere, have you?"

She glanced at the empty corkboard and cocked her head to the side. "No, sorry. I didn't realize they were gone. I'll keep an eye out. They've got to be here somewhere."

I left the cubicles and stubbed my foot on a hardcover book. Cursing beneath my breath, I picked it up and then eyed the shelves before me. Row after row of them sat bare. Between them were mountains of books just piled on the floor. How had anyone made this much mess in a single night?

Making my way into the children's section, I went to work. Many of the books had been damaged by the rough treatment. Broken spines, torn book jackets, and crumpled pages. Picking up a copy of *Alice in Wonderland*, I shook my head. The cover had almost been torn right off. Such a waste. If I ever met the person responsible for this atrocity, they'd meet the same fate as the phantom dog-poop dropper.

"The little heathens," I mumbled, as I closed the book and set it on a pile for repairs.

The re-shelving was a good distraction. I could do it in my sleep, which left me plenty of time to think about everything going on. Soon the kids would be back at school which would be good for them both. They needed to spend time with other people. Hopefully it would help take their mind off their father.

Conor didn't really understand what was going on but I was pretty sure Shay knew better.

He'd been gone for months. They were going to work it out sooner or later. I just didn't have it in me to break the news to them.

How do you tell your kids stuff like this?
You shouldn't have to.

I slammed the next book onto the shelf, a whole lot harder than I intended.

The divorce was going to take time to finalize, and he didn't seem to be in any particular hurry. He wasn't fighting me for custody of the kids, so I didn't want to push the point.

I sorted book after book, setting aside any that were damaged and in need of repair, loading them onto a trolley I found flipped on its side.

Sally caught up to me as I reached the fantasy section. And, angel that she was, she was carrying a piping hot cup of coffee.

She offered it to me. "I figured I'd find you here. Any excuse will do, huh?"

"In my defense, I did start in the children's section," I replied, reaching for the steaming mug of hot coffee.

Holding it up to my nose, I took a deep breath and savored the aroma. Even here in sunny Queensland, there was nothing like hot coffee to get you moving in the morning.

Fully air-conditioned at someone else's expense and surrounded by books, this job was normally heaven on earth. If only we could get Karen to retire, or have the stick surgically removed from her behind, things would be perfect.

Sally and I chatted and sorted, sipping coffee as we went. The library might have been trashed, but apart from the damage, it wasn't all that different from a normal day's work. Albeit there was a lot more of it to be done, and no readers in sight anywhere. While we toiled inside, some commercial cleaners gathered up the glass and not long after that, glaziers arrived and began fitting new sliding glass doors.

That was a perk of working for Council; tradespeople tended to respond quickly when the need arose. After all, the government paid its bills promptly.

Spotting a copy of *Magician*, I scooped it up and looked it over. Somehow, it had managed to survive intact. Little miracles. I set it on the shelf and with that patch of carpet cleared, I moved to the next mountain.

"We're making good time," Sally said, plucking a book off the top of the pile. "We're in danger of finishing this row before midday. What are we doing for lunch?"

My stomach let out a rumble. "I haven't had anything but a yogurt and that coffee so far today. I could use something a little more substantial."

There was a cafe around the corner, Luv A Coffee, that did a pretty good lunch. They made a mean risotto.

"Sounds like a cafe day?" Sally said, as if reading my mind.

I scooped up another book. Its cover was torn, and I set it on the cart. "Yep, I'm thinking a club sandwich with fries would hit the spot."

Lifting the next book, I paused. Lodged among the pile of trade paperbacks was a leather-bound book I'd never seen before.

In a library with tens of thousands of books, that may not seem unusual, but this was my turf. I'd handled every book here a dozen times, read most of them. The good ones more than once.

The leather-bound title was almost as thick as a bible. I picked it up, and a tingle shot through me. It was like I'd touched an exposed wire.

"Ow," I cried, pulling back my hand.

Sally looked up from the book she was shelving. "What is it?"

I turned my hand over, but there was nothing there. No papercut. Nothing.

Maybe I'd tweaked a nerve or something.

"A new book," I said, as I reached for it once more.

I was more cautious this time. When my fingers touched the worn red leather, nothing happened. Maybe I'd just imagined things. Pulling the book out of the pile, I studied it more closely. There was no bar code or blurb on the back. As far as I could tell, it didn't even seem to be a commercial publication. Turning it over in my hands, I examined the front cover. Its title had been etched with engraving tools into the leather.

It read simply, *The Otherworld*.

My curiosity was piqued.

In Irish mythology, the Otherworld was the name given to the unseen world inhabited by supernatural beings. A place of magical creatures like the Sidhe and ruled over by the gods. Some, my mother among them, believed the Otherworld could be reached by passing through portals beneath ancient burial mounds. Her desire to be further from them had brought her here to Australia. Just about as far as one could get from Ireland.

"Looks like an interesting book," Sally said. "Have you read it?"

I shook my head. "I've never seen it before."

I opened the back cover, looking for a chip or insert with the library's name on it. Perhaps we'd received it from another branch.

The inside of the back cover was completely blank.

"I don't think it's one of ours," I replied. "No markings. Perhaps someone left it here by mistake and it got swept up in the mayhem."

I fanned the pages and then let the book fall open. The entire page was covered in neat lines of handwritten script. I turned the page. The next one was the same. Flipping through the book, I found hundreds of pages of handwritten notes.

It wasn't a book at all. It was a journal.

Many of the pages had a heading in bold. They read names like Kelpie, Basilisk, Gruffs, Unicorns, Banshees, and the Loup Garou. I recognized some of them as mythical creatures, but others were new to me. Several of the pages had fold out plates, covered in sketches of the creatures, except they weren't portraits. Each of them was covered in markings highlighting the creature's anatomy and weaknesses. It was almost as if it was a hunting manual for creatures of fable.

Even more unusual was the fact that it was in English, not Irish, Gaelic, or Latin. It didn't seem that old either, but it had been meticulously prepared. Creating this journal must have taken hundreds of hours work. The research must have taken hundreds more.

If I wasn't working, I'd have loved to spend more time reading this odd little tome. I couldn't afford for Karen to find me slacking, so I tucked it into my handbag.

Sally shot me a look.

"It's not one of ours, and I just want to take a closer look. I'll bring it back to lost property when I'm done. It will be a day at most. Maybe two."

Sally laughed. "You're insatiable."

I pointed my finger at her. "Says the pot to the kettle. If this was the latest Colleen Hoover, you'd be all over it like a rash."

"No, I wouldn't... because I've already read it."

I laughed as I helped her to her feet.

"It came out three days ago," Sally said. "What's a girl to do?"

Before I could answer her, a scream cut through the still library.

I ran to the end of the row of shelves and tracked the sound.

One of the glaziers dashed across the foyer toward us.

"Run!" he shouted at the top of his lungs.

Beyond the freshly hung glass doors, a lumbering gray shape thundered toward the library.

The creature had to be at least ten feet tall. It reached the stairs, grabbed the steel handrail in one meaty hand, and wrenched it right out of the concrete.

Swinging the handrail like a bat, the creature charged inside, straight through the fresh panes of glass.

Chapter 3

Sally shook as she pointed at the door. "What is that?"

"I don't know," I answered, my breath coming in short bursts. "But we have to get out of here."

Tiles cracked beneath the creature's bulk as it paused in front of the library's welcome board. Stretching to its full height, the creature scanned the library, clearly looking for something. We ducked behind the rows of freshly re-shelved books.

The creature had to be almost ten feet tall. Its skin was mottled grays and blues, and it had a thick coat of shaggy tangled fur running down its back. Its head, easily the size of my torso, had a sharp angular shape to it, like a rectangle but for the two big ears jutting out of it. The ear on the right had a silver ring hanging from it the size of a basketball hoop. The beast's yellow eyes darted back and forth. Slow and ponderous though it might be, it was moving with purpose.

Searching for something.

"It looks like those trolls you see in children's books," I whispered to Sally. "Don't you think?"

Sally's lip quivered as she nodded, unable to manage a word.

I didn't know what to do. My mother had told me about creatures that lurked beyond the Veil, but I'd never expected to see one in our world.

The troll prowling the library looked pretty real to me.

It let out a gurgling belch accompanied by a fetid yellow-green mist, and I thought I might be ill.

The library had a fire exit in the rear. Grabbing Sally's hand, I pulled her toward it. We were going to have to circle around the bookshelves and creep along the periphery of the library. If we made a run for it, the creature would almost certainly see us. I might have been wearing flats, but there was no part of me that wanted to race and find out which of the two of us was quicker. Forty might be the new thirty, but no one had told that to my calf muscles, and cardio was the only thing I felt as strongly about as I did Karen. They were both the devil.

I guided Sally back along the row of books. She felt cold and clammy to the touch and didn't seem to be thinking straight. My heart hammered in my chest. With each step, I prayed the freshly re-shelved titles would help mask our presence.

"What is going on here?" Karen's abrasive tone carried through the library.

"Oh no," I groaned, my heart sinking.

I stole a glance through the rows of books. Karen strode out of her office to confront the disturbance. When she saw the beast, she stopped, rooted to the spot. She screwed up her nose at the stench, even as she began to tremble.

For once in her life, Karen didn't have anything to say.

The troll eyed Karen like she was little more than an hors d'oeuvre. Cocking its head to the side, it opened its mouth in eager anticipation.

I willed her to run, but she cowered in place as the towering creature loomed over her.

I couldn't blame her, but if she didn't move, she was as good as dead.

If half the stories my mother had told me were true, the troll would think nothing of devouring Karen and adding her bones to its stash.

The creature's jaw distended, and it let out a throaty grumble as it started to raise the steel handrail.

Karen's eyes followed the creature's hand but still she didn't move.

"She's dead," I groaned, staring at the stubborn old woman.

An hour ago, I would have given everything I had to get Karen out of here. But not like this. No one deserved this.

"I can't believe I'm even considering this," I whispered, as I turned to Sally. "Run for the fire exit. I'll meet you there."

"What are you doing?" Sally hissed as I let go of her.

I just waved her off before jogging back the way we'd come. If I stopped to answer her, what little courage I had mustered would dissipate.

Racing out of the row of bookshelves, I collected the book trolley laden with damaged books and pushed it before me. The wheels squeaked and rattled in angry protest as the cart and I picked up speed. The troll's head swung up, its eyes locking on me and the squeaking cart.

"Run, Karen!" I shouted as I came screeching down the main thoroughfare of the library. My breathing was ragged, as I ran out of carpet and onto the tiles. The noise from the cart became deafening.

Looking down at the damaged books, I whispered, "Forgive me."

I gave the cart a shove, letting go, sending it sailing past Karen toward the troll's legs.

The troll swung the raised handrail at the encroaching cart.

I grabbed Karen by the arm and yanked her after me. "Let's go!"

I risked a look over my shoulder. The troll's makeshift club struck the book trolley, flipping it. Books, loose pages, and cover jackets went everywhere.

The cart tumbled over itself, before colliding with the creature's leg. There was a sickening crunch as the steel cart struck muscle and bone. The troll's maw dropped open. Saliva, at least a cup full of it, splashed down onto the tiles as it shook its head in outrage. Its yellow eyes turned bloodshot as their focus shifted to me.

Its knee joint was bent at an unnatural angle, but the troll wrapped its hand around the joint and wrestled it back into place with a bone chilling crunch.

Karen and I ran for our lives.

The cart had bought us a few moments, but that was it. The troll lumbered forward, its leg somehow still able to support its tremendous bulk.

I was out of options. Dragging Karen with me, I ran like the devil himself was after us.

The troll lurched after us, its gait a little uneasy as it nursed the wounded leg.

The tiles beneath it splintered, spiderweb-like cracks shooting out from under its feet. The troll had to weigh more than my car, and all of it was muscle and bone.

Beside me, Karen huffed and panted. The hundred meter sprint clearly wasn't her specialty. Not that I could talk. She had two decades on me and was still managing to keep up. Either that or she was relying on the old adage that she didn't have to outrun the troll; she just had to outrun me. Knowing Karen, I wouldn't put it past her. At least her legs seemed to have caught up with her brain.

Ahead, Sally and the glazier waited by the open fire exit, frantically waving at us. I risked another look over my shoulder. The troll was gaining on us with every step. They might have been awkward loping strides, but it was much taller than us. One step of his equaled three of ours.

Sweat ran down my brow as I realized the truth. We were never going to make it. Not like this. Not in a straight sprint.

I pushed Karen ahead of me. "Run! Call the police."

"The police?" Karen's tone rose. "What are they going to do about *that*?"

"Just go," I bellowed. "Before I change my mind."

I made sure the troll was watching me as I broke off and ran into the children's section. The creature looked from me to Karen, but it was clearly capable of bearing a grudge as it ignored the easy prey and kept right on my tail.

If I couldn't outrun the troll, I was hoping I could lose it in the maze of shelves. At worst, I hoped the shelves would slow it down.

If I could shake him in the maze, I could double back or meet the others at the door. I grabbed the heaviest book I could find, a children's encyclopedia, and lobbed it backward over my shoulder. The weighty text went wide, landing on the floor, and the troll continued to lumber after me.

I reached the end of the first row of shelves and turned down the next aisle. I was almost halfway down when the creature stopped at the head of the row. I stole a look over my shoulder, as the lumbering brute smashed the end of the shelves with his club. Books flew off the shelf all around me.

One of them hit my ribs. Another struck me in the side of the head.

My foot hit the slick surface of a laminated book and shot out from under me. I went down like Steven Bradbury's competitors at the Winter Olympics.

I hit the carpet hard, the jolt of the impact starting in my well-padded rear but carrying up my spine, undoing all the good work my chiropractor had done yesterday. I winced in pain as my lower back screamed its vehement protest.

Nora, you idiot, what are you doing? People with chiropractors don't antagonize trolls; they read about them in books. They also tend to live a lot longer for that very reason.

I groaned. Today really wasn't going how I had planned. I wasn't cut out for this, but I wasn't ready to give up either. I'd survived Judas. I wasn't letting some lumbering brute from the Otherworld get the better of me.

I rolled onto my knees and started to rise when a shadow completely obscured the light from overhead.

Sighing, I raised my head.

The troll loomed over me. Its big gap-toothed grin salivated wildly at the prospect of its next meal. If Karen was an hors d'oeuvre, he must have thought he hit the jackpot. There was a little more of me to meet his appetite.

My brain screamed at my muscles to respond. I had to do something. My hands were shaking, both from proximity of the troll and the pain spasming through me from my fall.

Ten feet of what I'd previously believed to be a fictional creature towered over me. It was even uglier up close, and it reeked like canned fish and rotten eggs. Around its girthy waist, it had a leather belt with what appeared to be pieces of bone pierced through it. Over one shoulder, it wore the hide of some furry creature that tapered over its back. The thick shaggy coat of gray fur melded with the troll's own hairy torso. It was difficult to tell where one ended and the other began.

The troll studied me. It didn't appear to be in any hurry. Why would it? It was the predator here and I was the prey.

My sacrifice had bought the others time. I hoped help was on its way. The police station was only around the corner. They should be here in moments. I just needed to keep moving.

I couldn't die here. Not like this. Not now. My mind filled with images of Conor and Shay. Who would take care of them if something happened to me? Would they be forced to live with Judas? Not this side of hell freezing over, and here in Queensland, nothing ever froze over.

"Listen here," I groaned, hoping I sounded more intimidating than I felt. I didn't have to kill the troll. I just had to outwit it. I staggered to my feet and willed all the power I could into my hands. Icy mist poured out of them, streaming toward the floor.

"If you touch me, I will freeze your ugly ass right there where you stand. For eternity you'll be the troll who got his ass beat by Nora Byrne."

The creature cocked its head to the side as if considering my threat. Its bloodshot eyes watched the mist pour from my outstretched hands.

I felt self-conscious. I was a human manifesting arcane talent. That should have at least caused him to reconsider his decision to have me for dinner. But instead of considering me a threat, he was curious.

It was as if he was judging me. He saw the icy mist not as a threat, but as a physical manifestation of what little power I actually had.

I felt his judgment, and it irked me.

What did he know? Surely no more than I did.

At least that was what I was hoping. If I could get him to see me as a threat, maybe he'd back down. Maybe he'd scurry back to whatever hole he'd crawled out of.

What was a troll doing in the middle of Beenleigh anyway? We had snakes, spiders, and a dozen other venomous creatures, but we didn't have trolls.

It craned back its head and let out a throaty gurgle that was unmistakable.

He was laughing at me. That was as unsettling as it was unwelcome. It meant the creature could both understand me, and at the same time know I posed no real threat whatsoever. After all, chilling a beverage and turning a ten-foot troll into an ice sculpture required far different levels of power, and certainly far more than I could manage. I was a party trick pretending to be an elementalist, and he seemed to know that.

Oh, crap.

The troll cast aside the handrail which clattered against the bookshelf beside us and advanced on me.

Did he think so little of me as to throw away his weapon? I racked my brain for answers and remembered the stories mother had told me as a child. Trolls weren't afraid of ice, but they hated fire.

No wonder the beast thought I was hilarious. I might as well have threatened it with a well-cooked meal. I needed fire, but the closest source of heat was the kitchen and it lay on the other side of the towering troll.

If I could dart past it, maybe I could reach the kitchen. Big as it was, it seemed awfully clumsy. I just needed to duck beneath those lanky arms.

The troll reached out, not a crushing blow aimed to reduce me to a smear on the carpet, but to grab me. I threw myself to the side, landing awkwardly on a mountain of freshly dislodged books.

The troll caught nothing but air, but he snatched his hands toward me again, aiming to scoop me up.

"Duck!" a voice bellowed. It was thick and heavily accented.

I rolled out of the path of the troll's descending arms. I tried to scramble to my feet but the voice behind me shouted, "Stay down!"

I glanced over my shoulder and found a man standing behind me.

He had to be at least two of me wide, and wore a black leather jacket, jeans, and heavy combat boots. A thick coppery brown beard several inches long concealed much of the lower half of his face and his equally coppery brown hair was pulled back into a simple topknot.

"Teine!" he bellowed in a thick, unmistakable Scottish accent.

A flame flickered to life, floating in the air between his hands. It grew larger with every passing second.

He was a wizard. A real one.

Chapter 4

The man parted his hands to accommodate the growing inferno.

The troll lumbered right for him but he stood his ground, his brows furrowing as a bead of sweat ran down his face. The inferno was the size of a basketball. With a flick of his wrists, he sent the ball of fire hurtling at the troll.

The charging troll raised its arm to try and shield its face.

Fire washed over the troll's arm, bathing it in searing heat. It let out a roar that rattled the shelves and reverberated through my chest. It leaped at the wizard.

The landing shook the building.

I scrambled to my feet, my heart racing.

Smoke started to fill the aisle. Several stray embers had found their way into the books that were littered everywhere. At least three small fires had started. If I didn't do something, they would surely spread to the other shelves. The whole library could go up in flames.

At the end of the row, the wizard deftly dodged the bone-crunching blows.

Raising my hands, I summoned what power I could muster and doused the first pile of books with icy sleet. An angry hiss filled the air as frost met fire. As I poured on my power, I managed to smother the flames out of existence.

One down, two to go.

Panting with the effort, I checked on the struggle behind me. The wizard had drawn an immense machete from somewhere and was locked in hand-to-hand combat with the troll.

The machete would open a wound in the troll's thick muscled hide, but no sooner had it opened, than the flesh knit itself back together, sealing the wound.

I doused the other fires, but not before they had destroyed dozens of books. Here and there small embers scorched the fibers of the carpet, but thankfully they hadn't caught.

Down the aisle, the wizard appeared to be losing ground against the troll. Sweat ran down his brow and into his coppery beard as he hacked at the creature.

He needed help, but what could I do? Other than get beaten to a messy pulp, of course.

Setting aside the smoldering around me, I looked for ideas. Putting out the fires would do me little good if the troll was able to kill my would-be savior. I hunted for something to use as a weapon. Spotting the discarded handrail, I stooped down for a better look. One end of it was a sharp and twisted mess where it had been wrenched out of the concrete.

I grabbed the handrail and tried to stand. It wasn't nearly as easy as the troll had made it look as he brandished it about with one meaty fist. Using both hands, I managed to raise it to my waist and set off after the troll.

The wizard ducked under one of the troll's clumsy blows before opening a wide gash in the creature's thigh. Like the others, it began to knit closed, but slower this time. It was like the creature was fatiguing.

With a gurgled grunt, the troll delivered a savage backhand with a speed that caught the wizard flatfooted. The strength of the blow sent him flying clear into the nearby bookshelf. He struck it with a thud before collapsing on the ground. The troll lumbered after him, then raised its boot to crush the life out of him.

Huffing like Bran on one of our summertime walks, I clung to the handrail and rushed at the creature's back. Noting the thick hide and his shaggy fur, I aimed for the creature's flank, just below where I hoped his ribs might be, and drove the handrail home.

The twisted piece of steel pierced the troll's hide, burying itself a foot deep in the creature's guts.

A tortured shriek escaped the troll, buying the wizard the few moments he needed to roll away from being stomped. The troll's armored boot descended, missing the man's head by a whisker.

The troll reached around and wrapped his massive hand around the steel rail.

Leaning into the rail, I gave it everything I had, trying to force the bar up into his heart. But the troll was simply too strong. With one meaty fist, he wrenched the handrail out of his flank. It was coated in a thick sheen of greenish-blue blood.

At least the troll could bleed.

I should have been focused on the rail I was still holding onto rather than gloating. The troll tried to wrench it completely away from me. I held on, not wanting to give him a weapon he could use to beat my brains out.

I was lifted off my feet and swung unceremoniously through the air as the troll pivoted. When my tired wrists gave out, I let go of the handrail.

I flew the better part of six feet before belly-flopping onto the library floor. The thin layer of cheap carpet didn't do a whole lot to cushion the blow. The wind burst from my lungs, my ribs protesting the pain as I lay there groaning in agony.

What was I thinking?

The troll closed in on me to finish the job. The black-leather clad wizard interposed himself between me and the enraged creature.

"*Teine!*" he chanted.

Flames flowed up the machete's blade until the entire length of the machete was alight.

The troll paused, its eyes glued to the flickering flames.

Then it raised its burnt left hand like a club ready to crush the wizard to death. I needed to move, but I couldn't. My muscles ached and protested the abuse I'd subjected them to, and I was exhausted. I just didn't have anything else left in me.

The wizard lunged forward, feinting a blow at the creature's left leg. When the troll tried to step backward, the wizard darted forward and changed the angle of his strike, bringing the fiery blade across the troll's stomach. Flaming steel opened the troll like a piñata, spilling entrails and gore down the troll's front.

It was the most disgusting thing I'd ever seen come out of a living being—and I had changed gastro nappies.

I tried to fight the bile as it rose but seeing the spaghetti-like mess of his intestines, I lost it. I vomited right there on the floor of the library.

The troll teetered forward, falling to its knees, its regenerative properties stayed by the flames. With both hands gripped firmly on the machete's handle, the wizard swung at the troll's neck. The burning blade carved straight through bone and sinew, its head rolling off its shoulders and landing with a heavy thud on the floor in front of me.

Wiping my chin, I managed to scramble out of the way as the troll toppled forward and landed in what was left of my meager breakfast.

I was glad I'd already been ill. I didn't think I had anything left in me, but the sight of the headless troll pushed that theory to the brink. I retched and gagged but managed to keep it together.

"You all right?" the wizard asked, his Scottish-accented voice deep and gravelly, that made each word sound like it had an extra syllable in it.

I looked at him, his beard and jacket sprayed with blue troll blood. His skin had a thin sheen of sweat on it as he wiped some of the troll muck off his face. He looked how I felt: exhausted. My gaze reluctantly made its way back to the headless corpse beside us.

"I am not all right," I whispered, brushing what I hoped was sweat from my forehead.

I didn't look at my hand. I didn't want to know.

"That thing was trying to kill me." I pointed at the troll. "There's fire and blood everywhere. How could I be okay?"

The wizard shrugged as he wiped his machete on the troll's back and tucked it into a scabbard across the small of his back. "I figured it was more polite than telling you that you look like hell."

"Thanks," I answered, pushing a mess of tangled hair out of my face. "I guess it's the thought that counts."

The man bent down and examined the troll, kicking it with his boot a few times to test for any reaction.

"It's dead, right?" I asked, tucking my hands in my pockets to stop them trembling. "I mean, its brain is no longer connected to the rest of its body."

"That does tend to present a problem," he replied, without turning around. "Though that never seems to stop politicians."

I found myself smiling and didn't know what to say. The library was quiet, and an uneasy awkwardness settled in the air as I watched him work.

"You never can tell with trolls." He poked the creature's scorched arm. "Amazing regenerative abilities and this one was ancient."

"You say that like someone who has seen one before."

"More than one," he said as he wandered over to the end of the row and picked up a leather satchel. "Not my first. Doubt it will be my last. Though usually you wouldn't see them in these parts. Too hot for an ice troll."

I took a deep breath, hoping it would help relax my racing heart. He might have just saved my life, but he had an infuriating talent for speaking without actually saying anything informative. As if I didn't have a thousand questions that needed answering. Like who he was, how he knew about trolls, and how he could work freaking magic like Harry Potter, if Harry Potter would ever morph into a ruggedly handsome Scotsman.

I couldn't muster a fragment of the power he had unleashed. Wizards weren't common here. It was Beenleigh, not Bag End.

"What are you? A wizard?" I asked, trailing him back to the troll.

He laughed, a thick rumbling chuckle that started in his belly.

"I was never a card-carrying member of the Arcane Congress, if that's what you're asking. They don't hold much sway here in the Wilds."

"But you do wield magic?"

"Can't get anything past you," he replied, as he slid a leather pack off his back and set it down beside the troll.

His sarcasm wasn't helping my mood any.

"What do you mean, the Wilds?"

Beenleigh was a rough neighborhood some days, but wild seemed like a stretch.

He shrugged as he stooped down beside the troll's body and started searching it. "In my world, there is everywhere the Arcane Congress exerts its influence—Europe, America, some parts of Asia—and there is everywhere else. Either due to too few people, or sheer distance, our high-minded wizarding bureaucrats can't be sodded keeping an eye on things. Those places are the Wilds, and Australia is about as wild as they come. Best the Congress will do for you is put a bounty on creatures like this and hope someone is brave or stupid enough to do something about it."

"So, you're a..." I let the sentence trail off, hoping that perhaps I could lead him to a direct answer for once.

"Bounty hunter," he replied, like that was normal. Sure. It was about as normal as an ice troll in our public library.

"You have talent, too," he replied. It was a statement rather than a question.

I didn't know where that put me in his eyes, so I didn't answer him.

"I saw the trick with the ice." He rummaged through the troll's possessions as if he was searching for something.

"Neat trick. Wrong choice for an ice troll but we work with what we're given, I suppose."

It was hard to tell if that was an insult or a compliment. The bounty hunter had a way of keeping me off balance, and I didn't like being on the back foot. I'd thought I was better at holding down a conversation than this, but then again, I hadn't managed to hold down my breakfast. Perhaps it was the fact that he was a man, a handsome one at that, if you could see past the troll guts. He had a rugged exterior a woman could certainly appreciate, and my eyes were doing a little too much appreciating. My brain wasn't thinking clearly. Damn hormones always firing up at the worst times.

The bounty hunter looked up and caught me watching him.

"How is it you aren't on their radar?" he asked.

"Their?" I replied.

"The Arcane Congress. Normally they track talent, but you're not on our list either."

I looked down at my hands and sighed. "They tested me when I was younger, before my mum moved here from Ireland. Minor magical talent, not worth training, I guess."

He regarded me, raising an eyebrow, and then shrugged. "Probably for the best."

"Hey, what's that supposed to mean?" I asked, placing my hands on my hips.

"It means you're better off without them meddling in your life," he replied. "Wizards are a law unto themselves."

With that, he scooped up the troll's head and started jamming it into his massive knapsack.

I wanted to turn away, but I couldn't. It was like watching someone try to thread a needle with a roll of dog food. "What on earth are you doing with that?"

"Like I said, I'm a bounty hunter. I need proof if I want to be paid."

"You get paid... for *this*?" I gestured at the now headless troll.

"Wouldn't do it for free," he replied as he somehow managed to fit the troll's head into the bag which seemed a little too small. "It pays the bills, most days anyway. Today ought to be a good one."

"How much does it pay?" I asked, my curiosity getting the better of me.

He looked at the knapsack. "An old ice troll from the Otherworld? The guild should be able to get ten grand for it, on a good day at least. The Arcane Congress likes to be seen preserving order."

"Ten grand." My eyes almost rolled out of my skull. That much money for what had only been a few minutes work? That was crazy. If I could make that sort of cash, my rent woes would disappear overnight.

"Yep," he replied, tossing the bag over one shoulder. "Maybe more if I can sell what's left of its brain to an alchemist somewhere."

Gross. I didn't want to think about that one any more than I already had. I'd seen more than enough of the troll's insides to last me a lifetime.

"It pays well when there is work around. Can be a bit feast or famine, though. That's why I moved here. Lately seems to be all sorts of activity in these parts. Mind you, a hunter's life expectancy is a bit rubbish. If you chase these creatures long enough, one of them is going to punch your ticket eventually."

His accent told me he was Scottish, but from the way he spoke, he seemed like he'd been around town a while.

"So, you live around here then?" I said, fishing for more info.

"Lately," he replied. "But I best be getting out of here so the boys in blue can do their job."

He looked down at the troll's body and whispered the same spell he'd used earlier.

Flames poured from his outstretched hands. I leaped backwards as fire bathed the troll. The hunter was relentless, smothering the creature in scorching heat. It took less than thirty seconds to reduce what was left of the troll to ashes. In his effort, he burnt clear through the carpet to the concrete slab beneath. I was frankly a little shocked that the fire didn't spread, but I had a feeling in my gut that he had something to do with that.

"This isn't legal, then?" I asked.

He laughed. "One of those 'don't ask, don't tell' kind of things. Police aren't stupid. They see things they can't explain all the time, but they're so busy dealing with mortal felons, they appreciate us taking care of the more magical threats that find their way into the neighborhood. As long as people don't get hurt, and we clean up after ourselves, they leave us alone. Call it professional courtesy."

Sirens approached the library and the man looked over his shoulder.

"Time to go," he said as he glanced at me. "You're handling this better than most, but if you'd prefer, I can wipe your memory. Help you sleep a little better tonight."

Wipe my memory? He could do that?

I held up my hand. "No, thanks. This thing just tried to kill me. I'd rather remember that, just in case."

"In case you meet another ice troll?" he asked, raising an eyebrow.

I made some martial arts gestures that I'm sure looked far more awkward and corny than I'd intended.

"You never know when you might need it," I replied, trying to sound more collected than I felt.

"Suit yourself." He slung the knapsack over his back as he looked toward the exit.

"You saved my life. Aren't you going to at least tell me your name?" I asked as I slid sideways into his path. He'd have to go through me if he wanted to slip out the back door.

He let out a low breath as he weighed his options. "Alasdair. Now, can you please get out of my way?"

"I'm Nora," I replied even though he hadn't asked. "Just one more question. How does one become a bounty hunter?"

Thoughts of the ten thousand dollars still floated through my head.

"You find the Camp," he replied, shifting his weight from one foot to the other. "If you can't get that far, you have no business being a hunter."

"Where should I start?" I asked. Going door to door would take months, and I didn't have that kind of time.

"It's here in town," Alasdair replied. "Apart from wanting to be a hunter, you seem to have a good enough head on your shoulders. If it's meant to be, you'll get there, but don't even think about following me. I have other errands to see to."

He turned sideways and shuffled past me. As he headed for the back door, he looked over his shoulder. "But if you have a shred of common sense in that skull of yours, you'll forget you ever met me."

He hurried toward the fire exit. I considered following him, in case he'd been lying about where he was headed, but I realized that in the chaos, I had dropped my bag. It had everything in it: my wallet, my keys, and my phone. I couldn't afford to lose any of them.

Small embers glowed where Alasdair's magic still simmered. I didn't have time to play firefighter now, and judging by the sirens amassing outside, the real deal was already here.

I hobbled back to the fantasy section as fast as my battered body would allow and found my handbag still resting against the shelf where I had dropped it.

I slung it over my shoulder. I was closer to the entrance than the fire exit and with the troll gone, it seemed just as good a choice as any. Catching my breath, I trudged toward the front door, weaving my way through a sea of broken glass.

No sooner had I reached the outside stairs than a pair of police officers ran up to me. I recognized one of them as the same young officer who'd been there earlier that day, his brow furrowed with concern.

"Ma'am, are you okay?" he called as he rushed toward me.

"Call me ma'am again, and you'll have to arrest me for assaulting an officer," I replied, mustering a smile.

After the troll, I doubted I could take a wet paper bag and was grateful when he put his arm under mine and helped me down the stairs. It was the closest thing to any action I had had in months. I let my mind wander as he escorted me down the stairs to where a group of staff were gathered along with police and firefighters from the local stations.

Karen was there, and so was Sally.

"Nora," Sally called out to me. "Thank God you're okay."

As her eyes traveled down my body, so did mine. I was a total mess. *Okay* was the last thing I felt, but I was alive and that had to count for something.

I nodded slowly. "I've seen better days."

For the first time in my memory, Karen's face softened a little. Less angry principal, more concerned home room teacher.

"I'm glad to see you made it out, dear." She leaned in closer. "I was worried that thing got you."

"He tried, but I'm all right." I didn't mention the bounty hunter or the part he had played in things. If I hadn't seen it with my own eyes, I might not have believed it myself.

"Well, you head on home and get some rest. I'm sure you could use it after all this excitement," Karen said. Her polite way of telling me I looked just like I felt.

She wasn't wrong, but I'd used up all my sick leave taking Conor to specialists last month. Any time I took off, I wasn't getting paid for.

"No, no, no, I'll be fine. Besides, I need the hours. I'll stay here with you guys and clean up."

Karen rested a hand on my shoulder. "Sorry, dear, this place is going to be a crime scene. We're not going to be able to work until they're finished."

"What?" I groaned. I was already behind on my rent. I needed the work.

"Don't worry, we'll make sure you get paid for the day." Karen sighed. "But I fear we're going to have to close up until the police and insurers see to things. We could all be in for a little unpaid leave."

"Close up? Unpaid leave? Karen, I need the money."

She nodded, giving me a sympathetic frown. I wasn't used to seeing that expression on her.

"We all do, dear, but our budget funding has been cut for the third year in a row. I've only been taking half pay for the last six months to try and keep everyone else's hours up. This is just the straw that broke the camel's back."

I was utterly shocked. She hadn't mentioned anything, least of all that she'd been taking half pay so that we could keep our hours. No wonder she'd been so crabby about me being late.

I felt awful for all the things I'd muttered about her beneath my breath. At the same time, I felt good for not letting the troll squish her like a bug.

"Head on home, dear. I'll call you and let you know how things go here. I'll try to keep our hours going at half pay, at least as long as I can."

I looked down at my feet and fought back the urge to cry. I'd survived an ice troll, only to lose my paycheck, at least half of it. The timing couldn't be worse.

The landlord was already knocking down my door for our overdue rent. If I didn't come up with a solution, and fast, I was going to be evicted.

What was I going to do?

Chapter 5

I stood there in slack-jawed disbelief while I tried to hold back tears. Part of me felt a little ungrateful. After all, I was still alive, but this situation sucked. My day had gone from bad to worse, and it was showing no sign of letting up anytime soon.

Going to my mom for money was the last thing I wanted to do. At forty, who wanted to let their lifelong single mom prop up their finances?

"The poor thing is still in shock," Sally said, placing a hand on my arm. "Nora, let me give you a lift home."

"Don't I need to give a statement or something?" I replied, looking at the handsome officer who'd helped me out of the library.

He shook his head. "No, we're all good here. We got what we needed from your colleagues. If we have any follow up questions, we'll be in touch."

"B-but the fire," I stammered, trying to collect my thoughts.

"The firies are in there now, dealing with it. I'm sure they'll work out what started it."

Part of me wanted to scream that magic had started the fire. I was there. But as I looked at the faces of the first responders and my colleagues, I realized what was going on.

If they took my statement, they would have to record what I said and no one wanted to be the police officer submitting a report saying that an ice troll had rampaged through the public library. Those who still thought magic and the supernatural world were a hoax tended to frown on that sort of thing. And police officers with a shred of intelligence overlooked those particular details, at least when it came to their reports. No one wanted to scuttle their own career.

I followed Sally to her car, a beat-up old Honda Civic. We passed a pair of firies in full gear heading for the library. I hoped they were overkill. There had been little more than smoke and embers when I'd made my way outside. The poor library couldn't catch a break.

Sally pressed a button on her keys and the car's locks popped open. The old door could use a little WD40, and it gave a weary creak as I opened it. I collapsed heavily into the seat. All of me hurt, and a part of me thought I was going to need every minute of the month off to recover from the beating the troll had dealt out.

"Still worried about the time off?" Sally asked. "Things a little tighter than you've been letting on?"

I clutched my bag tight to my chest. I didn't want to burden Sally with all my troubles. She had plenty of her own. The Honda Civic had been second hand when she got it, and that was at least ten years ago. She had been driving it almost as long as I had known her. She spent her spare cash on her first love, books, not the rust bucket that got her to and from work.

"I guess I thought it would be easier," I said. "Things were pretty comfortable when we had two wages around the house. Now I've eaten through my savings, replacing the stuff he took when we separated. Meanwhile, Judas keeps raking in the cash and has hired some high-priced lawyer and is taking his time settling things. Who knows what he's up to?"

"What an ass," Sally said as she pulled out of the car park. "I never did like him, you know. Always thought you could do better."

That brought a little smile to my face. Sally was a good sort; always made an effort to cheer up others.

"Yes, if I can just find an eligible CEO with some spare discretionary income, who's good with kids, and a tiger in the sack, I'll be fine."

The chance of finding that in little old Beenleigh was practically zero. But it didn't pay to dwell on that. Sally had found her partner here, and so had I. Or at least I'd thought I had. Perhaps I could do it again, or maybe like Mom, I was better off on my own.

"You and me both." Sally laughed. "In the meantime, I guess I'll have to stick with Mike."

The pair had been high-school sweethearts. In spite of what she might say, Sally would be lost without him.

I laughed, but my heart wasn't in it.

My mind was already occupied considering what I was going to do about my situation. There was a big part of me that wanted to roll into bed, but that pity party was going to have to take a backseat. I was a mother first. No matter how crappy my day had been, there would be things to do at home.

There would be dinner to cook, chores to enforce.

The thought of the kids brought a smile to my face. If it hadn't been for Alasdair showing up when he had, I might not be going home. That was something to be grateful for.

And I'd met Alasdair. That made for two things. Maybe one and a half, when he opened his mouth.

Yes, definitely at least one and a half things that had gone my way. The bounty hunter fascinated me. Clearly, he knew a lot more about the world of magic than I did, but that wasn't saying much.

Unlike other people in my life, namely my mother, he seemed more than willing to talk about it. Every time I raised my talent with my mom, she'd make an offhand comment about my father and dismiss the discussion. She'd grown rather adept at it over the years, and I'd learned to let it go.

With what I was going through with Judas, I couldn't really blame her. I didn't want to talk about him any more than she seemed to want to talk about my father.

Sally turned onto my street. It was a quiet little cul-de-sac, but it certainly had its eccentricities.

The property on the corner housed our local would-be pharmacists. They never ventured outside and it showed with their overgrown lawn. A steady stream of people came and went at all hours of the night. The rumor mill said that Len was either a drug dealer or that he was running a brothel. If either were true, it was the most poorly kept secret in the neighborhood. He'd been reported to the police a number of times but, like used tape, nothing seemed to stick for long.

As we rolled down the street, we passed Mrs. Grobinsky with her little toy poodle. The pooch was convinced it was a tiger and made far more noise than its little frame should be capable of, much like its owner. Mrs. Grobinsky was the largest gossip in the postcode, always prying into other people's business. She'd tried to talk to me about the divorce at least twice, but I didn't feel like having my dirty laundry aired at her weekly bridge club, so I'd ended the conversation as politely as I could while trying to prevent Bran from eating her little breakfast-sized dog.

I wondered if they were the dynamic duo responsible for leaving the foul-smelling land mines on my lawn each morning. If it was, she needed to get that pooch to the vet. There was something seriously wrong with its bowels.

As I thought about it, though, I couldn't recall seeing her out and about at that hour. Mrs. Grobinsky was in her fifties and a widow, which left her all the time in the world to loiter, gossip, and play at her imagined title as unelected president of our local neighborhood watch.

As we eased past, she eyed me warily. Strange, given the obvious drug deal that was occurring on the street corner a hundred meters away. I would have figured there were far more interesting things going on than the fact that I was home from work early, but apparently not.

I smiled and waved, with all five fingers extended, despite the temptation to do otherwise. She managed an awkward nod, giving me the sort of forced smile you reserve for your least favorite cousin, and waved with the enthusiasm of a limp fish in a bucket that had run out of water.

Sally rolled to a stop in front of my place, and I reached for the door handle.

"Thanks for the lift home, Sal."

"So we're not going to talk about what happened in the library?" she asked.

I let out a sigh. "What do you want me to say? You saw it as well as I did."

"A troll in downtown Beenleigh," Sally whispered. "I didn't think they were real."

"I've only heard about them in fairy tales, but that thing was as real as anything I've ever seen," I replied, my nails pressing into my scalp as I pushed my tangled hair back out of my face.

"How did you get away from it?" she asked, popping the car into park. "And why didn't you mention it to the police?"

I shrugged. "The troll was gone. I didn't want to give them a reason to shut us down for longer. What did you say about it?"

Sally shook her head. "Nothing, figured they would have thought I was crazy. Karen didn't mention it either, at least as far as I heard."

That was a relief. Less chance that I'd be called in to answer follow-up questions at the station.

She leaned closer to me. "Where did it go?"

"Can you keep a secret?" I asked, not sure how much of the experience I wanted to share.

Sally's ears twitched. She was every bit as curious as Mrs. Grobinsky but was also the most loyal person I'd ever met. She wouldn't share my secrets with the world.

I fiddled with the strap on my bag. "A man showed up, right after you and Karen slipped out. I thought the troll was going to kill me, but he got in the way. He killed it and disposed of its body, too. As far as I could tell, he was some kind of wizard."

"A handsome stranger shows up and saves you from a rampaging troll and you don't lead with that?" Sally asked, her jaw dropping a little.

"Who said he was handsome?" I replied.

"The corners of your mouth perked up when you mentioned him." Sally smiled. "And you didn't deny it either, so I'm betting I'm right."

She wasn't wrong.

"I guess he was," I replied, "right up until he cut off the troll's head and jammed it in his backpack. I've been out of the dating game for a while, but my mum always taught me to avoid men who collect severed heads."

Sally shook with laughter. "You sure know how to find them."

"I'm not looking," I shot back as I pulled on the handle and opened my door. "Thanks again for the lift home."

"You call me if you need anything," she said. "Anything at all, okay?"

I nodded and shoved the door shut behind me. We both knew I was never going to call. I'd find a way to make ends meet, and I'd do it without burdening my friends.

I waved as Sally pulled away and turned to find Bran waiting for me at the fence.

His doggy head was cocked to one side, his eyes fixed on me with obvious concern. I looked down and had to agree with him. I was in considerably worse shape than I had begun my day.

I wandered over to the fence and ruffled his ears. "Hey there, big guy. It's been a long day. How are things around here?"

Bran nudged his head up against my hand.

He was a good boy.

I slipped through the gate and sat on the grass beside him. My big dog rustled up against me with enough enthusiasm to almost bowl me over. I wrapped my arms around his neck and pulled him tight against me, rubbing his flank.

It didn't matter how crap my day was. Bran was always happy to see me. Tired though I might have been, I trickled a little chill out of my fingertips as I rummaged through his fur.

Bran looked at me with those big doggy eyes that told me he hadn't forgotten my promise.

"Still looking for that walk, huh?" I asked.

Before I could say another word, Bran bounded around the back of the house and reappeared a moment later with his leash in his mouth. I grinned; his enthusiasm was infectious. I might have been tired, but a promise was a promise and my house wasn't on fire, which meant Mom had things under control. At least for the time being.

I clipped the leash onto Bran's collar, and we made our way down the street. I picked the opposite direction to Mrs. Grobinsky and headed for the dog park. At this point, Bran was walking me, and I figured I'd take the chance to let him off the leash so he could run and play to his heart's content.

As we walked, I couldn't help but think about the house. The landlord had given me three weeks to come up with the missing payments. At half pay, there was no way I could meet them, that was just math, but I did have time on my hands.

Perhaps I could get another job.

I found my mind wandering back to Alasdair the bounty hunter. Reaching the dog park, I let Bran off the leash. He took off across the grassy field.

Alasdair had been pretty emphatic that I should forget his existence, but it was hard to dismiss the sight of him lopping the head off the ice troll. Some things just stuck in your mind. That included the payday he'd talked about as he'd stuffed the troll's head into his pack. Under normal circumstances, I'd never have thought of myself as capable of that kind of work. But I was a mom, and I wasn't capable of watching my children become homeless, not under any circumstance. Not while I had a breath still left in my body.

The problem was, Alasdair hadn't exactly been recruiting. I had no idea where one started other than his cryptic directive to find the Camp. Whatever that was. All he'd said was that the Camp was in town. Beenleigh is not a big city, not by any stretch, but it wasn't a two-street town either. There were plenty of commercial buildings, shopping malls, and other crannies in this concrete jungle that it could hide in.

And what if it wasn't in the town itself? What if the Camp was an actual camp? It could be anywhere. There wasn't much by the way of campgrounds in Beenleigh, other than the tents and caravans parked on the slopes of the Beenleigh Showgrounds. No one paid them much heed, so there were plenty of people squatting there.

Maybe that was what he'd meant? Perhaps tomorrow I'd wander down and check it out.

Bran finished his lap of the park and bounded back to me.

I tried to stretch, and my back protested the beating I'd taken at the library.

"Maybe the day after," I muttered, mostly to myself.

I walked Bran over to the drinking fountain and used the tap to fill the empty dog bowl beneath it. Bran lapped eagerly at the fresh water while I ruffled his ears.

"Okay, you little camel, let's get home and give Gran an early mark."

I popped the leash back on his collar and let him lead me home. With my faithful hound dragging me along, all I had to do was lift my feet and he would make up the difference.

Whoever said forty was the new thirty was a flaming liar.

Resting my hand on the gate, I tried to catch my breath as I let Bran back into the yard. Reaching into my bag, I felt around for my keys. I slid them into the lock and let myself in.

I found my mother napping on the couch. My daughter and her friends were still bouncing around upstairs. I looked for Conor, but he was nowhere to be found. At this hour, with no schoolwork, he was likely to be on his computer, trying to squeeze in as many rounds of games as he could before dinner.

I reached for my mother's shoe and rustled her gently. She startled awake, her blue eyes settling on me as she rubbed the sleep out of them.

"Wait, what. What time is it?" She groaned as she glanced at her wrist.

"Just after three," I replied, settling down on the couch beside her.

"That's early, isn't it?" she asked as she sat up. "What's going on?"

"Rough day at work," I replied. "Someone robbed the library last night and trashed it."

Mom placed a hand on my knee. "The little cretins."

"And while we were cleaning up, it was attacked."

My mom blinked furiously as she tried to wake up. "The library? Attacked? By who? Are you okay?"

"I'm fine, a little bruised but fine," I said as I sank back into the lounge. "You're not going to believe this, but it was a troll."

My mother shot to her feet. "A troll? What sort of troll?"

"That's your question?" I asked, shaking my head.

"What do you mean?" she replied, fixing her hair.

"I tell you a troll was rampaging through suburban Beenleigh and your first question is, what kind of troll?"

"Yes, dear," she replied, checking the windows. "I have been telling you about the Otherworld all your life and you've brushed me off like a crazy old woman. Don't expect me to coddle you now that you've finally experienced it for yourself."

She had a point, and I didn't know how to reply.

"Answer the question," she said. "What kind of troll was it? What did it look like?"

I dredged through my memory, trying to recall the specifics. "Well, it was blue and gray and the fur on its back was all matted and tangled. It had big yellow eyes that grew more bloodshot when it was injured."

"Ice troll," my mother said. "Creature of Winter. That's not good."

"There's a time when a troll *would* be good?" I asked, more to goad her than out of any real curiosity.

"If you'd ever endured a plague of pixies, you'd know better. Trolls can certainly help with pest control, but there's a reason I chose to come here, to Australia. There is so much you don't know about the Otherworld."

"Like what?" I asked, my curiosity piqued.

She glanced around, as if looking for eavesdroppers. "Like the fact that it intersects with our own based on shared climate, emotions, and sentiment. I picked sunny Queensland because the places it borders in the Otherworld are the domain of Summer. We are as far as one can get from Winter and the malevolent creatures that inhabit his domain. For an ice troll to be this far from home, it can't be an accident. Summer and her guardians should have dealt with it long before it reached here."

"Well, you needn't worry—it's dead," I said, hoping to calm her down.

"How?" Her tone grew sharp.

My mother was the one person I didn't have to worry about thinking I was crazy. After the lifetime she had spent rattling on about the Otherworld, she was more likely than others to take what I said at face value.

"A man showed up. He said he was a bounty hunter, though he seemed to be a wizard. He managed to kill the beast. Well, we killed it. He did most of the work, but I helped. Mostly as a distraction, I guess."

"Foolish girl." My mother had a way of making me feel twelve again. It was a tone I loathed. "What were you thinking, taking on a creature like that?"

"I was thinking that I don't want to die," I replied.

My mother let out a long breath, her brow furrowed, the wrinkles at the corners of her eyes deepening. "You look like you've had a long day, dear. Why don't I stay here for the night? I'll help watch the kids while you get some rest."

Empathy wasn't an emotion I was used to in my mother, but I wasn't going to turn down help after the day I'd had.

"Sure, Mum, that would be great. I've just got to fix something for dinner first."

My mother followed me into the kitchen and snatched the apron that I picked up off its hook on the side of the fridge.

"If I have to eat it, I'll be helping."

It wasn't the greatest endorsement of my cooking, but it was probably warranted. Mom was an excellent cook; a skill I'd never managed to acquire. She had always been far more interested in telling me about the Otherworld than how to cook a steak or season things properly.

"What were you thinking of making, dear?" she asked in a tone that mixed condescension and care in a ratio only an Irish mother could master.

"Spaghetti," I replied. "Don't judge me. It's cheap and easy. We have mince in the fridge and plenty of pasta in the cupboard."

"I'll take care of it. Why don't you head upstairs, have a shower, and cleanup? You don't want to worry the kids."

She was right. I didn't want either of them to see me in this state.

I made my way upstairs, my tired muscles protesting the effort as the sound of pots and pans being rummaged through rang out from the kitchen.

Shay and her friends were still bouncing around her room with an energy that frankly made me downright envious. I passed Conor's door and paused. I was worried that if I went to my room, I might not come back out and I couldn't do that without checking in on my little artist.

I cracked the door open, just an inch so he wouldn't see me. Conor's room was wallpapered with his sketches, each blu-tacked to the walls in neat rows. In the corner, Conor sat at his PC, his headset over his ears, a look of intense concentration on his face.

"Healer?" Conor called into the mic. A cluster of indecipherable responses was muffled by the thick padded earpieces.

I smiled and closed the door. He seemed to have a far easier time interacting with others without the pressure of being scrutinized by them.

In my bedroom, I closed the door quietly, tossed my bag on the bed, and made my way into the bathroom. I threw my clothes into the laundry hamper and wondered if I wouldn't be better off burning them. I doubted Napisan would get the troll out of them, but it was worth a try. It would certainly put the stain remover to the test. I hobbled into the shower and let the warm water blast away at my aching muscles.

Right around the time I reached lobster status, I dragged myself out of the shower, toweled off, and grabbed some pajamas before collapsing on my bed.

Perhaps a little nap wouldn't hurt. I just needed to set an alarm. Reaching into my bag, I went for my phone, but my hand brushed against something cool and smooth. Pulling the bag onto my lap, I yanked out the foreign object, only to find myself holding the red leather-bound journal.

I'd totally forgotten about it in the chaos, but something in the book seemed to call to me. A shiver ran down my spine as I slid my hand over the elegant patterns on its cover.

"I guess the nap can wait," I whispered as I pushed my bag to the side.

I rested the journal in my lap and opened it.

Chapter 6

The Otherworld was scrawled across the first page of the journal in large cursive script. As I smoothed the page flat, a wisp of power running through my hand and up my arm. I shivered at the sensation and the realization that this was no ordinary journal. There was something arcane about it.

Magical artifacts could be dangerous, particularly when you had no idea of their origin, or what purpose they had been created to serve. I knew I should close the tome, but after the events in the library and meeting Alasdair, I just couldn't bring myself to do it. I turned the page.

A word of warning.

That was the simple heading written neatly across the top of the next page. Perhaps it was a sign, one I should heed. My heart skipped a beat.

I read on, and it was almost as if I could see the images in my mind as I devoured the words of the author.

Beyond the Veil that divides the mortal world from the supernatural, there are many realms. All have borne many titles over the years. As one who has walked them, I have often found the simplest is the best. In my mind, there is our world and the Otherworld.

Who had written this? There was no byline. I felt like I was reading an explorer's journal as I continued.

Along the periphery of the Otherworld, bordering closest on our own, is the land of Faerie. Home to the Sidhe courts and inhabited by a multiplicity of creatures, Faerie might be the closest to our realm geographically, but should nonetheless be regarded with extreme caution. The creatures that inhabit it are both self-serving and duplicitous, eager to ensnare mortal beings in their unending intrigue.

The Sidhe are masters at seduction, offering mortals what they truly desire in exchange for a price that is seldom what it seems. Mortals who treat with the Sidhe are destined to be ensnared by them. While the Sidhe will always fulfill the letter of their agreements and obligations, the spirit is at best neglected and ofttimes perverted entirely. The Sidhe should only be approached when the need is dire. Our interests are inextricably linked and they can be relied on to act in their own best interest. Otherwise, they are best avoided.

I turned the page eagerly. It read like a non-fiction treatise but could just as easily have been someone's fantasies scrawled in a notebook. Was it fiction? Or was it something more?

My gut and the lingering trace of power in the journal, told me it was much, much, more.

The author continued. *Should you lack the foresight to ignore my warning, consider carefully with whom you deal. Among the Sidhe there are two courts. The words majestic and terrible could be used to describe either and both.*

Summer shines bright as the sun at noon day, but her beauty should not be allowed to deceive you, for the source of her warmth and beauty is power and power will corrupt a man as readily as anything else in this world.

"Good thing I'm a woman," I mused as I turned the page.

Winter. Cold, dark, and unyielding, the forces of winter are savage and sharp. Their interest in humanity is limited by the utility they can extract from us. Winter's value seems to lie only in tempering Summer's ascension, as an unending summer could spell doom for us all. Together the courts are Yin and Yang, balancing each other in a perpetual struggle for dominance.

Should either triumph, or gain the upper hand for a prolonged period of time, our world would suffer. While mortals think we are the masters of our own destiny, our fate is tied to the Otherworld more closely than most understand. The seasons of our planet are tied inextricably to the zenith and nadir of Summer and Winter. Global warming might have first been considered alongside the industrial rise of men, but it can just as readily be tracked to a decades-long rise of heat as Summer bolsters her power and prominence.

Winter, not easily left behind, has extended his icy hand to embrace the earth. The results of their struggle? An increasing and erratic global upheaval, dramatic natural disasters of growing intensity. The struggle rages on.

The arrogance of man; no sooner do we put a label on something than we think we comprehend it. The Sidhe struggle against each other and we feel the brunt of their conflict. Should one triumph over the other, it could spell cataclysm for us all.

But beware, should you try to temper the elements. Once you choose a side in this eternal conflict, you can never return to neutral ground.

I turned the page. Somewhere in the back of my mind, I was aware of the spaghetti being served downstairs—I could smell the garlic and basil from my bed—but I simply couldn't bring myself to put down the journal.

And so I read, page after page, barely cognizant of the sun setting outside my window, the first sign of the hours that had passed since I picked up the Otherworld journal.

The pages were filled with descriptions of the courts of the Sidhe, or at least what information and opinions the author had managed to garner and organize.

He spoke at length of the creatures that belonged to either kingdom and their place in it. At least their place as far as the author understood. He—and I was fairly sure the author was a man—gave his opinion throughout the manuscript on a range of otherworldly politics. Whoever had written the journal appeared to have spent extensive time in the Otherworld.

How had he managed such a feat? Was he an explorer of sorts? The wizarding equivalent of Captain Cook or Magellan as he charted the lands beyond the Veil. The journal seemed surprisingly silent on how he had managed to reach the Otherworld, or how he had survived its many perils. Perhaps the absence of a description as to how to traverse the Veil was best explained by the consistent warnings left throughout. It seemed to be his opinion that only a fool, and a desperate one at that, would willingly engage in such an undertaking.

My interest only grew as I turned the pages one after another, after another.

I flicked on my bedside light, as I banished any pretense of going to sleep and read long into the night. I didn't know when my consciousness gave out, but when I awoke, the journal was resting open on my chest, where it had fallen when my weary hands finally let go of it.

I stretched and stifled a yawn as I tried to get up. My body let out a grumble of protests from yesterday's encounter with the troll but a rumble from my stomach silenced their protestations.

You're forty-two, Nora, not twenty-one, my inner voice muttered. *What were you thinking, trying to wrestle a troll?*

"I was thinking that I didn't want to die," I replied sharply, talking to myself like any sane woman would. I dragged myself out of bed, found my phone that had slipped off the bedside table. I checked the time. Seven a.m. I ought to go right back to bed and sleep away the day. After all, I didn't have to go to work today.

I turned to the red leather-bound journal resting by my pillow and thought back to my night's reading. In spite of the author's warnings, I found myself utterly intrigued with its contents. Part of me wanted to read more. As best I could remember, I'd barely made it a third of the way through. The Bible-like compendium was a wealth of knowledge. Or perhaps opinion. I really had no way of knowing what was what.

Personally, I had little experience with the Otherworld, bar my encounter with my friend, the troll. Perhaps I could raise the journal's contents with my mother and get her opinion.

I dressed and went downstairs, aiming to put an end to the rumblings in my stomach. Opening the fridge, I spotted the yogurt. I ought to eat something healthy, but I'd skipped two meals and the last yogurt I'd eaten, I'd seen again after it came back up.

No part of me was in the mood for yogurt. I found a bowl of cold spaghetti that had been cling-wrapped.

I pulled it out of the fridge, tossed the cling wrap, and popped the bowl in the microwave. Good old Chef Mike never let me down. A minute later, I was chowing into a bowl of warm spaghetti. Not the healthiest breakfast I'd ever had, but it was certainly hitting the spot. The combination of diced mince, rich, fresh tomatoes, and pasta with a touch of parmesan was heaven on my taste buds.

My mother could cook. Far better than I could anyway. I promptly devoured the entire bowl.

I stuck the bowl in the sink for later, my standard M.O. for procrastinating one of my least favorite household chores.

My mother appeared in the doorway.

"Good morning, sleepyhead," she said with a smile as she looked at her watch. "That was some nap."

"Morning, Mom. Spaghetti was great, thanks," I said, slowing my pace. "You didn't come get me for dinner?"

"I figured you could use the rest."

I felt a pang of guilt. I didn't particularly want to admit I'd spent the night reading rather than sleeping, but I didn't regret it. Reading *The Otherworld* had been the best escape I'd had in weeks.

"Where are the kids?" I asked. The house was far too quiet for this time of the morning.

"Shay went over to Cassandra's house to stay the night, and Conor was still on his computer when I went to bed. Judging by when I called it quits, I doubt we'll see him before noon. What are your plans for the day?"

"Well, with everything that happened at the library yesterday, I have some spare time but need work. Something to help make up for the fact I'm on half pay. If I fall any further behind on rent, they're going to evict us."

"Things are that tight?" she asked, pursing her lips.

"Yep, things are a lot tighter without that second paycheck to share the load. And in this market, I don't want to be looking for a new place to rent."

"You know, I could help with that," she said. "I have a little money tucked away. I've been saving it for a rainy day."

"I can't do that, Mum. I need to stand on my own two feet. If I can't do it now, I never will. Besides," I said, looking into those stubborn gray eyes of hers, "you're already doing more than enough by helping with the kids. Next week, they'll be back in school and I'll be able to focus my efforts on making rent. In the meantime, I was thinking of hitting the streets and finding out what other options are around."

My mother nodded. She'd been down the path I was walking.

Looking out the kitchen window into the yard, she said, "Not to worry, dear. I'll stay here for the day, in case Conor needs anything."

"You're the best." I gave her a hug. "I'll only be a few hours. Going to visit some local businesses, see if anyone is hiring. I'll be back as soon as I can."

"Take your time, Nora. I've got things here."

Her lips were pursed tightly and the crow's feet at the corners of her eyes seemed a little deeper than yesterday. Something was bothering her. I imagined my current circumstances likely reminded her of Dad. I wanted to ask, but she wasn't one to talk about those sorts of things. So, I patted her on the arm before heading upstairs. I slipped into my comfortable walking shoes, grabbed my handbag, and made my way back down the hall.

At Conor's room, I cracked open the door, allowing a sliver of light into the otherwise dark room. His curtains were drawn, but there seemed to be some light coming from his bed. Figuring he might have left his phone screen on, I ventured into the room. It took a moment for my eyes to adjust to the dark. The faint aura of blue light was coming from the head of the bed.

I stopped dead.

The light wasn't coming from his phone at all. It was coming from him. Or more particularly, from his eyes.

As he lay there, the blue hue seemed to be seeping through his eyelids as if his eyes themselves were emitting the light. My heart skipped a beat. What was wrong with my baby?

Racing over to the bed, I placed my hand on his head expecting some sort of fever, but it was cool to the touch. Power surged up my arm from the point of contact. It reminded me of when I drew on my own gifts. Only where my power felt like a trickle of energy, Conor felt like a river was coursing through him.

He has talent.

It was the only conclusion that made sense. But what was happening? Why were his eyes glowing, and how long had this been going on?

As a thousand questions stampeded through me, Conor's eyes flicked open and the light faded.

I recoiled in shock, and I wasn't able to get my legs beneath me before I backed right off the bed. I landed on my ass and found another one of yesterday's bruises.

"Mum?" Conor asked, his voice heavy with concern. "What are you doing?"

I picked myself up off the floor, feeling a little sheepish. I looked at my son, and all signs of the otherworldly light was gone.

"Sorry to wake you," I mumbled as I tried to work out what was going on. "I just wanted to check up on you before I went to work. Are you doing okay?"

Conor nodded, a smile spreading across his lips. I placed my palm on his head to check it once more. It was warmer to the touch this time. Part of me wondered if I had imagined the whole thing.

"Is Gran still here?" he asked.

"She sure is," I replied, pressing him to lie back down. "But you get all the sleep you need. She'll be downstairs when you're ready for breakfast."

I rose to my feet. I was going to have to talk to him about this, but not while he was half asleep. I thought back to my own teenage years, and the confusion my own talents had caused as they manifested. I'd just about flooded the bathroom when I'd frozen the tap while the faucet was still running.

The conversation was going to have to wait. I bent down and kissed him on the forehead. "Love you, baby."

"I love you too, Mum," he replied before snuggling down into his pillow.

Letting myself out of the room, I headed for the front door. Spotting Mom in the lounge, I called out to her. "Conor stirred. I imagine he'll be down in a bit."

"No worries. I'll fix him some breakfast."

I considered telling her what I'd seen, but she had reacted poorly to my gifts when they had manifested, so I decided to hold off. There was no point in alarming her until I knew what was going on.

"Have fun," I called before heading out the front door.

On my way across the lawn, I checked the side yard, but Bran must have been napping. I stepped over the pile of fresh dog poo sitting in the middle of my lawn and set off to find the Camp.

I hadn't lied to my mother, but I might have embellished my intentions. I didn't think she would be on board with my current plans, but if there was a place in town I could make ten grand off a single day's work, that would be more than enough to tide me over. It would take care of the rent and maybe help secure a pit bull of a lawyer to deal with Judas and his stupid attorney. I couldn't make do with pocket change. I needed real money, and I needed it quick.

Alasdair's words played through my mind. If the Camp was somewhere in town, then I was going to find it. It felt like a test; I doubted bounty hunters accepted job applications. Perhaps if I could find their lair that would go a way toward proving I could handle myself. Not that I should have to. After all, I had helped him with the troll.

My inner critic wasn't so easily convinced.

Yes, and you got tossed across the room before being sick all over the place. You're the picture of competence, Nora Byrne.

I held up my finger. "Shut up, you. No one needs Negative Nancy right now. Particularly me. Unless you have something to say about the Camp, you need to nick off."

They say talking to yourself is a sign of insanity, but I'd always found it cathartic. And apart from the negativity, I could use any help I could get.

What about the Showgrounds then? The thought returned, this time in Negative Nancy's condescending tone.

What could it hurt?

There were always carnivals passing through town, and the Showgrounds had a large transient population housed in a small tent city and a series of caravans clustered together. The Showgrounds and the surrounding land occupied a surprisingly large section of land near the middle of town and went relatively unnoticed in spite of the fact the police station was only a few streets away. It seemed the perfect place for people who didn't want to be found.

I made my way down the street, taking my time. I needed the cash, but I also needed to be thorough and to stay on my feet. After pushing it yesterday, I figured it was probably prudent. My body had limitations and if I continued to ignore them, I was likely to hurt myself. Whether forty was the new thirty or not might be in dispute, but my bruised ribs and aching back were realities.

Maybe I'd stop by the chiropractor too, show him what I had done with all his hard work.

"You've got a little tension in your shoulders, Nora," I mused to myself.

"You should see the troll," I countered, entertaining myself as I made my way through town.

I had a car, but it seldom left the garage. The three-year-old Prius might have been a hybrid but even with its fuel efficiency, it still cost more money than walking, so I tended to let it sit unless I was heading further afield. Like taking the kids to the beach for the day or making a run into Brisbane.

I passed the service station, trying to ignore the temptation to duck in for a morning coffee. Petrol station coffee was certainly the bottom of the barrel, but it might give me a little more pep in my step.

I glanced at the sign of a mug sitting in the window, decided I wasn't that desperate yet, and carried on my way. The Showgrounds sat between James and Milne Streets, nestled against the main roundabout in town, but took up more than half a dozen city blocks. It was made up of a large grassy arena where monster trucks and car shows operated whenever the circus wasn't in town. Beside the arena, on the long sloping fields, were a series of caravans, tents, and temporary structures.

I wasn't quite sure what I was looking for, but I wandered onto the grounds anyway. I made my way through the gates, passed by the field, and headed down the grassy hill. With no shows currently in town, the fields were empty. When I reached the first row of caravans, I found a woman loading laundry into the back of her car.

"Excuse me," I called to her as I approached.

She was a slender woman, dressed in jeans and a t-shirt with her sandy blond hair pulled up in a messy bun.

She took one look at me and went back to her laundry.

"What do you want?" she asked over her shoulder.

I took a breath, mainly to consider how I might ask my question without sounding insane. But I came up short and so I just threw it out there for her to consider.

"I was wondering if you've heard of anywhere in town referred to as the Camp. I'm just looking for directions."

"Can't help, I'm new here," she replied, in a tone that was utterly devoid of sincerity. "Only know my way to the grocery store and the laundromat. I don't know any more than that."

"Thanks, anyway," I replied. I barely made it five steps, when she called after me.

"You might want to try the Old One down by the pond. He's been here the longest, I think."

I looked where she pointed to a rundown caravan parked by a small, dirty pond. It was off on its own, isolated from everyone else. The grass around it was almost two feet high, but for the annex. The place had to be a nightmare in mosquito season. Pesky little bloodsuckers were everywhere after rain. Either he was immune from their oppression, or perhaps he just liked to keep others away. The mosquitos would certainly be an effective deterrent. The closest caravan to his had to be more than a hundred meters away.

"Thanks," I called back and made my way toward the caravan, hoping the Old One was around.

What kind of name was the Old One anyway?

It had to be a nickname of some sort. If he'd been around town a while, maybe he'd heard of the Camp. Or perhaps he'd met a bounty hunter in his time here. I wasn't sure that I liked my chances. I'd lived here for years and only met one yesterday. And if it hadn't been for the troll, I imagined I would still be oblivious to their presence.

But it was all I had to go on, so I picked my way through the long grass toward his caravan.

Dried paint flaked off its sides in great strips and the RV itself looked like it was from the sixties; white with a dirty brown highlight accentuated by a gold strip that had faded to an ugly yellow. A patch of grass a few meters wide had been freshly mown around the caravan, but beyond that the grass ran wild. The caravan had a small external sunroom attached to the side.

On closer inspection, I found it to be a weather-beaten gazebo from Bunnings, with walls attached. I used the word walls generously, as they were little more than tarpaulins that someone had zip-tied into place. Anything to keep the sun and its oppressive heat out, I supposed.

I looked down at my watch, mindful that it was still rather early, and crept toward the caravan.

"Hello?" I called. "Is anyone home?"

No one answered, so I made my way closer. I called out again, but still there was no answer.

I crossed the patch of freshly mowed lawn and paused at the gap in the tarpaulins that served as a doorway.

"Hello?" I said. "I'm looking for the Old One. Is he here?" A single twig snapped behind me. Before I could turn around, I felt the singularly unnerving sensation of a sharp blade being pressed into the small of my back.

Chapter 7

I didn't move an inch, which was harder than it sounded with my heart hammering in my chest. I didn't need to see the knife to know what it was. Even now I could feel its blade pressed against my back. All it would take was the faintest of pressure and it would pierce the fabric, and my skin.

My attacker was silent. I didn't want to do anything that could be interpreted as hostile. Whoever was behind me had me at a disadvantage, and the wrong move could get me killed.

"You wouldn't happen to be the Old One?" I asked, my voice wavering between hope and downright panic. Having a knife pulled on me was a new and altogether unpleasant sensation. As a librarian, I was used to dealing with late fines and overdue books, not being held at knife point. I tried to keep control of my bladder as I racked my brain for ideas.

If this was the Old One, a warning from the lady with the laundry might have mentioned how unreceptive he could be to visitors. I needed to find the Camp; I didn't need to be murdered and thrown in a murky pond.

The knife wielder took his time to answer, seemingly content to let me stew in my discomfort.

Sweat beaded on my brow, a product of both the heat and my nerves.

"What's it to you?" he answered, at last. His voice had an odd gurgle in it that was throwing me off a little.

"Well," I began, drawing a breath to calm my nerves, "one of your neighbors mentioned you'd been around town a long time. I was hoping you might be able to help me with some directions."

There was a gurgling rumble as he cleared his throat. "Never heard of a GPS, or a map?"

"The place I'm looking for isn't going to be on a map," I replied, trying not to match his gruff tone with my own.

"Perhaps that's because they don't want to be found," he said. "Much like some people don't want visitors."

"If that's the case, I'm sorry," I said quickly. "I didn't mean to startle you or trespass on your property. I was just looking for the Camp."

I threw the name out on a whim, hoping to at least get something out of him as I made my apologies and left.

The blade pressed so firmly against my back, I could have sworn he'd cut me.

"What does one of your kind want with the Camp?"

"One of my kind?" I asked. "You mean a woman?"

The knife was all that stopped me from turning and giving him a piece of my mind.

He let out something between a groan and a sigh before replying. "Answer the question, or I'll bury you in the lake. No one will ever look for your body there."

There was an unsettling certainty in his tone.

What the hell had I walked into?

Sweat ran down my face as I considered my next words carefully.

"I ran into one of their hunters yesterday," I began. "A man named Alasdair. He helped me with a troll that was rampaging through our library."

I had no idea if the man behind me even believed in the supernatural world but I had to tell him something, and the truth seemed like my best bet. When he didn't run me through, I figured he wanted me to continue.

"I'm looking for work, okay? I need the money and Alasdair mentioned it paid well. I'm not looking to cause any trouble. I just have bills to pay, ya know?"

If the Old One lived in a beat-up old caravan beside a swamp swarming with mosquitos, I had a feeling he knew a thing or two about money trouble.

The blade slowly withdrew. I let out a deep sigh of relief.

"So you fancy yourself a hunter?" he asked.

"I fancy myself a mother, and I have two kids to feed, so I'm willing to do what it takes."

He let out a gurgling laugh. "That's what you think, now. Only time will tell."

"So, you know of the Camp then?" I asked, figuring him for more than a hermit.

He knew what a hunter was. And the more I thought about it, the more I saw signs that I was right. The Old One had intentionally chosen the most isolated corner of a trailer park, with clear line of sight of any approaching visitors, and those who did make it, he greeted with a knife in the back. I hadn't just found someone who knew of the Camp. I'd found someone who was a member of the Camp. I'd found another hunter, like Alasdair.

"You want directions, do you?" he asked, but my gut churned as I realized I was nowhere near out of danger. I sensed the baited hook, and after the knife, I was more than a little wary.

"Anything you can give me that might point me in the right direction," I replied, playing along. I didn't turn around. If the man had chosen to hide his identity, he'd done so for a reason.

A mosquito buzzed around my head, and I tried to flick it away with one hand, its irritating buzz humming through the awkward silence.

There was a meaty slurp and the mosquito's buzzing vanished.

"Those who would find the Camp, must do so on their own. That is the second test," he muttered.

"What's the first?" I asked.

"You've met a hunter and lived," the Old One replied.

"But how do I find somewhere I've never been?" I asked.

Silence prevailed, and I found myself growing impatient. "Hello?"

When no one answered me, I turned around. The Old One was gone, having vanished as swiftly as he'd arrived.

"I guess that's all the help I'm going to get," I said to myself. "At least I know I'm on the right path."

I looked around the trailer park, snooping for any hints. The laundry woman who'd pointed me to the Old One was long gone, which was probably for the best. After the knife in my back, I wasn't sure I could be civil if I saw her again.

When I couldn't find any other clues, I decided to start over from scratch. The Camp's location was a puzzle to solve, and I was pretty good at puzzles.

Pulling out my phone, I found a map of the city. Focusing on the intersection at the bottom of City Road, the central point of the city, I began my search. To the south, we had the library, the police station, and the magistrates' court. A study of the bird's eye view had me mentally ticking off locations with which I was familiar. If I knew the tenant of the building, I crossed it off. If it was vacant, or I hadn't been there in some time, I left it blank.

Finding a bench in the shade, I sat quietly, working through the map and crossing off as many locations as I could, to save me having to door-knock the entire town. If the Camp was truly in town, it could well be hiding in one of those commercial blocks. If it wasn't, door-knocking the suburban streets was going to be like hunting for snow in summer. I'd be destined to fail. In fact, unless Alasdair answered the door, it would be utterly impossible.

Hopefully it wouldn't come to that.

As I studied the map again, I realized that I'd left out a crucial consideration. Alasdair had arrived shortly after the ice troll had appeared. Which meant that either he was just in the neighborhood at the time, or the Camp wasn't a great distance from the library. Perhaps I was judging a book by its cover, but Alasdair, with his machete and head-removing hobbies, didn't strike me as the loitering type.

Factoring in the distance someone might be able to drive in such a short time frame, I drew a circle on my map. If he'd been at the Camp when the troll had materialized, then the Camp had to be somewhere in this circle. I checked the circle for buildings I could rule out and examined the ones that were left. There were about twenty-five buildings whose tenants I wasn't familiar with. After all, I'd spent the better part of the last decade working here in town. I knew a lot of people, at least the ones who frequented the library or places I ate.

I took my phone and made my way down the street toward the first of the buildings I'd identified as a possible location for the Camp. Unfortunately, there was no other way but to try them, one at a time, and see what I found.

On James Street, I visited the first shop on my list. Its glass windows had been smashed and the door was locked with a padlock that had a thick layer of rust coating it. I peered through the broken windows and saw no signs of life. In fact, no one had been through here in a while.

I crossed it off my list and headed for the next, a two-story commercial premises, built around a small car park. Several of the tenancies had no signage.

I took a set of concrete stairs to the second floor. By the time I reached the top, I was huffing more than I would have liked, but I trudged on. After peering through the glass, I crossed them off my list. There was a craft store, a new accountant, and an empty tenancy that was utterly bereft of any sign of life.

The third address on my list was being fitted out for a new gym, so it too was a bust.

By lunchtime, I'd visited more than twenty of the addresses on my list and turned up nothing. I grabbed a meat pie. Not the heavenly goodness sold by Yatala Pies, but the cheap variety from a 7-Eleven I passed on my way through town. I lifted my well-earned lunch out of its paper bag and sank my teeth into the crisp pastry crust. It was warm and delicious, and I devoured the first half while consulting my map.

Continuing down the list, I realized I was nearing the end of the locations I'd marked and still hadn't found anything.

I didn't know what the Camp would look like, but if it was filled with people like Alasdair, I imagined I'd know it when I saw it.

Five more places on the list. Hopefully that wouldn't mean five more strikeouts. My optimism was starting to wane.

Why are you wasting your time like this? How are you going to hunt supernatural critters when you can't even find a stationary building?

I ignored my inner critic. I wasn't in the mood for her crap today. After finishing my pie, I hurried through the last five buildings on my list.

Five more misses.

I reached the end of my list and found myself outside the police station. As the sun beat down, I couldn't help but wonder where I had gone wrong. The Camp had to be here somewhere, right?

I did a slow circuit, hoping I'd missed something. On the other side of the road was the post office. The Camp certainly wasn't in there; that had been here as long as the town had been around and was one of the town's hubs.

I wandered through the commercial blocks surrounding the post office, looking for unusual storefronts or businesses with which I wasn't all that familiar. Maybe I'd crossed something off prematurely.

But things remained bleak. I visited every business, knocking on the doors of those I didn't know well. All of them appeared to be legitimate enterprises.

Descending the stairs from the second floor, I plonked myself down and caught my breath. I'd been at this for hours and I hadn't found a whiff of the Camp since leaving the Old One.

What was I doing? I couldn't even walk around town without needing to catch my breath.

What business did I have considering becoming a bounty hunter?

"I don't have any other choice," I muttered.

While I'd been searching for the Camp, I'd kept my eyes open for other 'help wanted' signs, but there didn't seem to be a lot of job opportunities in our sleepy little town, so I might as well keep searching. I stood up as an old Holden pulled into the vacant lot beside the building. The lot seemed to serve as a carpark for the building beside it. I didn't know why, but something in my gut told me to take a closer look.

While my inner critic might have been a complete witch, my gut had never let me down.

I wandered over to the lot and examined the single-story brick building it was nestled against. The sign out front read Transport and Main Roads, the Aussie equivalent of the DMV. I had taken my driver's license test here when I was a teen, but that had been a lifetime ago.

That was when it hit me. Transport and Main Roads had moved years ago. I'd had to go across town to renew my car registration just last month. Yet another bill I couldn't particularly afford to pay, but likewise couldn't afford to ignore. If it had moved, what was here now?

I eyed the faded old signage as I made my way around to the front of the building. There was a pair of overgrown bottle brushes that hadn't been trimmed in years. I picked my way past them to an old sliding glass door that was dirty and covered in dust and smudged fingerprints.

The glass door slid open as I approached, revealing the same big empty office I'd been intimidated by when I'd taken my test for my learner's permit. A row of cubicles stretched along one wall, and an office sat out back.

Somewhere inside, a chime rang, announcing my entrance. No sooner had it cut off than a voice called out from the back.

"TMR's across town. Sorry we haven't pulled the signs down yet."

My heart skipped a beat as I recognized the thick, Scottish accent. I stepped further inside. A kitchenette was tucked in the back corner, and standing by the kettle, cup in hand, was Alasdair.

He looked up, his eyes meeting mine, and his face fell.

"Sweet mother of mercy, it's the vomit comet," he grumbled, to himself as much as to me.

Heat rose in my cheeks. I wasn't going to live that one down.

"I don't suppose you're here to renew your driver's license?" he asked.

I shook my head, my heart beating faster and faster as I realized I'd made it.

"You just don't give up, do you?" he replied, dropping a bag into his teacup as he headed to the fridge to pull out a container of milk.

"Consistency is a virtue," I replied, hoping my smile would win him over.

"Only if you're not a screwup." Alasdair poured a splash of milk into the cup.

Gee, he could be an ass. I ignored the taunt and pressed on. "So this is it? The Camp?"

It wasn't much to look at, but then, looks could be deceiving.

"No, it's the local brothel. I've just stopped by for a tea and a tumble," Alasdair said before he took a sip of his scalding tea.

"I'm sure your right hand will be glad to get the night off," I replied, crossing the room. "If I can just wade through your masses of adoring courtesans, I have a few questions."

Alasdair sighed as he set down his tea on the kitchenette's bench. "You smart ass."

He appeared to be smiling, but with that thick coppery beard, it was difficult to tell.

"This place looks like a normal office. What's with that?" I asked. "And where is everyone else? I figured there would be other hunters here."

"We like to be discreet, and it works, for the most part," he replied, ignoring my second question.

Before I could press the issue, the door set in the back wall swung inward, providing a straight view into the car park out back. Then a large frame filled the doorway. The newcomer had a hood pulled up over his head and wore a veil over his face. I assumed it was a *he* on account of his size and the style of his clothing. He had to be at least six feet tall. Unlike Alasdair with his thick chest and broad shoulders, the newcomer was all lanky limbs. I tried to meet his gaze, but the veil made my eyes swim. It consisted of several pieces of fabric pulled across his face, leaving only a small gap where his mouth was.

"I see you made it," the newcomer said, pulling the door closed behind him. His voice had the same familiar gurgle as the voice I had encountered at the Showgrounds.

"The Old One," I whispered.

It was a statement, not a question. I wasn't forgetting someone who had pulled a knife on me anytime soon. Now that I was seeing the Old One for the first time, I realized just how much danger I'd been in. The Old One had wicked long arms, and with their considerable reach, if he'd wanted to kill me, I wouldn't have stood a chance.

"Wait, you two have met?" Alasdair shook his head like someone who had been set up.

The Old One craned his head toward the kitchenette. "Yes, some loudmouth gave her the name of the Camp and she found her way to my home. Any idea who that might have been?"

His lips smacked together as he spoke. It was both unusual and unsettling.

I couldn't help but feel a little proud of myself. The Old One had sent me packing with little help, but I'd still found the Camp.

"So that's the second test. Is there a third?" I asked. "What's a girl got to do to be a hunter?"

I hoped my nervous enthusiasm would defuse the awkward tension between the Old One and Alasdair.

Alasdair shook his head. "You can't be serious."

"Why?" I asked. "I held my own against the troll, didn't I? If I hadn't stabbed him with that rail, he might have stomped your pretty little face flat."

The Old One let out a rumble of laughter, and Alasdair turned a similar shade to his beard.

"I had everything under control," he replied as he looked me in the eye. "Held your own? You drew a little blood. Big deal. Then you got your arse tossed across the library and spilled your guts at the first sign of his."

The Old One turned to me, and I could feel his gaze, even through the veil that obscured his face. He was waiting for an answer.

"You're not wrong," I said, "but I still helped, and I bought you enough time to kill that bloody troll. I've come back for more."

"She has both spirit, and guts," the Old One said.

"I know. She spilled them all over the floor," Alasdair added. He seemed intent on discrediting me, but the more they both spoke, the more I was beginning to realize they were not both hunters.

Alasdair certainly was, but the Old One wasn't. He gave off an air of authority and from watching the two of them argue, I was beginning to suspect that he was in charge around here.

Which meant Alasdair's opinion mattered little if I could sway his boss.

"Come on," I pleaded. "I need this, and from the look of this place, you're a little short on manpower anyway."

"Not that short," Alasdair scoffed, raising his cup to his lips.

"I seem to recall you talking about a rise in unusual activity in these parts. Are you telling me there's not enough work to go around? Or are you trying to keep it all for yourself?"

"He said that, did he?" The Old One stared at Alasdair. "Aren't you the Chatty Cathy?"

The Old One raised a gloved finger and waggled it at Alasdair before turning to me.

"Normally he isn't that talkative. Interesting."

"What does that mean for me?" I asked.

"That I'm inclined to give you a shot," the Old One answered, putting his arm around my shoulder. "See what you make of things."

There was an odd odor about him. Now that I was closer, and not fixated on a knife in my back, I couldn't help but notice he smelled like damp wool. Or perhaps that was just his attire. It was unusual, but then again, so was almost everything about him.

"You can't be serious," Alasdair barked, repeating himself.

"I'm deadly serious," the Old One spat back, pointing at the wall. On it hung a large cork noticeboard, and beneath it, mounted in simple brackets, were a series of gold coins. Each was small enough to fit in my palm, and there were more than a dozen of them. Beneath each was a picture.

I made my way over to the wall and, as I studied the pictures, I recognized many of their faces. They were all members of our community.

"What is this?" I asked.

"The Fallen," the Old One replied, a melancholy note in his voice.

Tom Cosgrave had run the bakery around the corner from the library. I'd eaten there twice a week until he'd passed away in a car accident. Or so I'd thought. Had he really been a bounty hunter? That explained the Mercedes he drove. He'd always said business was good. I'd just assumed he was talking about the bakery.

The more I looked, the more faces I recognized. I'd noted their passing with sadness, but never known the truth. I couldn't remember how they had all died, but I felt fairly sure several of them had been reported as car accidents. Which was a high road toll now that I thought about it.

Was that simply a cover?

The rightmost star had a picture beneath it of Levi Toa. He'd been one of Shay's teachers. He'd died last month, the result of a house invasion gone wrong. It'd been a terrible tragedy. He too, it seemed, had been a bounty hunter.

"Those we've lost in the line of duty," the Old One explained. "Seldom does a bounty hunter go out any other way."

My breath caught in my throat. I didn't know what to say. With a pay packet the size of what Alasdair had described, the job obviously had its risks. I just hadn't spent long enough thinking about what they might be.

I looked down at the faded carpet and wondered what I was doing here.

"Having second thoughts?" Alasdair asked, striding over from the kitchenette. "This job isn't for the fainthearted, or those with something to lose. Find some other way to make ends meet. You don't want to be the next coin."

I let out a sigh. He had no idea just how much I needed this job.

Lifting my eyes back to the coins, I realized that three of them had the same dates beneath them. Three hunters had died on the same day.

"What happened here?" I pointed at the coins.

Alasdair glanced over his shoulder at where I was pointing and spat. "None of your damn business."

I stepped back, surprised by the sudden change in his temperament.

I couldn't help but wonder if the money was worth the risk. As I stood there, my eyes drifted to the noticeboard above. On it were pictures of a handful of different creatures. None of them was human. Each was numbered: one, two, three, four, five, six. Beneath each was a description and a dollar value. The first was a leering creature that seemed almost humanoid but had a hooked nose, tapered ears, and a white beard. A dirty red baseball cap was turned around backwards on his oddly-shaped head.

The description beneath it read simply, 'The Red Cap. Bounty $100,000.'

My eyes bulged at the size of the bounty. That was almost two years' wages at the library.

The bounties ranged from the immense one listed under the Red Cap, to the sixth place which read, 'Malicious Fairy. Vandalizes School. Bounty $500.' Unlike the others, the picture above it was blank, or at least it seemed to be. On closer inspection there was a smudge-like blur passing across it.

These had to be active bounties.

Most of the amounts would be more than I made in a month at the library. I wouldn't have to worry about making rent for months.

My heart pounded as I made my decision.

Clearing my throat, I asked the question that was burning in my mind.

"What do I have to do to take one of these?"

Chapter 8

Alasdair laughed, the rich throaty rumble filling the room. In the library, I had found his laugh endearing. Now that I was the object of his mirth, the sound was quickly wearing on my nerves. Particularly after I had passed their silly little test and found the Camp.

"You can't just walk in off the street and take a bounty, lass," Alasdair said. "Even the least of those creatures will maul you if you get in their way. This is a trade to be learned, not a charity. You must apprentice to someone who knows what they're doing, or you won't last a day."

"Unfortunately, we only have one Master Hunter who would be available for such tutelage," the Old One added. "And he's a grumpy old Scottish bastard. I doubt you'd find him pleasant company."

"Don't even think about it." Alasdair set down his cup.

I wasn't sure whether he was talking to me, or the Old One, but I needed this job and I was just about to protest when the Old One intervened.

"Think about what?" the Old One asked, cocking his head to the side. "I'm in the habit of giving the orders around here, not taking them. Remember your place."

Alasdair stiffened, pointing his finger at me.

" You want to saddle me with Sally Homemaker here? She won't last a day."

"I lasted yesterday, didn't I?" I snapped.

"You survived," Alasdair replied, looking down his nose at me. "Don't mistake luck for skill, or competence. It's that sort of thinking that will get you killed."

He turned to the Old One, addressing him like I wasn't even there. His tone was more deferential this time. "Look at her, Master. She's been favoring her hip since she walked through the door. She's likely to blow her hip at the first sign of combat."

"Hey," I interjected. "I'm forty-two, not sixty-five."

Alasdair ignored me. "If someone is going to watch my back, I need to be able to rely on them. Otherwise, I'm better off alone."

"I can do pain," I replied. "I have given birth, twice."

The Old One chortled. "Certainly a glutton for punishment, aren't you?"

Turning to Alasdair, he rested a gloved hand on his shoulder. "I am inclined to give her a shot. I have a good feeling about this one."

"That's what you said about the last one," Alasdair growled. "He lasted all of three months, before the arrogant little sod went after the Red Cap. Now he's dead, and his wife is in a psychiatric institution. Heaven forbid you have a bad feeling about someone."

Three months. That was how long my predecessor had lasted.

I shuddered. My eyes rested on the photo of the hook-nosed creature occupying the top of the bounty board. A hundred thousand dollars was a lot of money, but you couldn't spend it if you were dead.

"I didn't have a good feeling about him," the Old One replied. "I said he had talent, and beneath that facade he was a psychopath. Using a monster to kill monsters was a healthier outcome than what might have occurred, had nature been left to run its course."

The Old One looked at me. "She is different."

Alasdair turned to me. "You said it yourself. You've got two children. That's two very good reasons to turn around and walk right out that door. If you insist on following through with this, I can't make you any promises. No one can. Who will care for your children if you're dead?"

"If I can't put food on the table and keep a roof over their heads, I'm not caring for them now."

Alasdair leaned on the table. "She can't be reasoned with. I'm sure she'll be a right pain in the arse to teach."

"No more than you were, I'm sure," The Old One said, his voice rising in its inflection.

Well, that explained their unusual dynamic. The Old One wasn't just the boss; he was Alasdair's mentor.

"How long are you going to hold that over my head?" Alasdair asked.

"Until the day you die," the Old One replied, letting out a wheeze. "May it be in your sleep, many years from now."

"Not bloody likely," Alasdair said, "and you know it."

"So it's settled then," the Old One replied. "Nora, you will accompany Alasdair and learn to be a hunter. Learn well, child, because he is right—there is no room for error here. Your next mistake could cost you your life, and I don't need any more coins on my wall."

As morbid a warning as it was, I couldn't help but smile. He was actually giving me a chance. What that entailed, I wasn't yet sure, but I had my foot in the door.

A klaxon-like siren reverberated through the confines of the building. I ducked, grabbing at my ears to prevent the din from deafening me. It sounded like an old air raid siren and was emanating from a rusty apparatus hanging on the back wall of the office.

"What on earth is that?" I shouted over the racket.

"It's the *aláram tairseach*," the Old One said, his voice weary and dry. "It warns us when the Veil has been parted within the city limits."

The Veil was the divider between our world and the supernatural realm. My mother had been lecturing me about it since I was a child.

The Old One trudged toward the office at the back of the Camp. He pushed open the door and the klaxon rattled in its mount.

Alasdair followed, and so did I.

The door led into a small boardroom. As the Old One passed through the door, he waved a gloved hand through the air and whispered something I didn't quite catch. The alarm abruptly stopped, and I was able to uncover my ears.

The boardroom was dominated by a large table covered by a miniature model of a city. It was not unlike those models architects used for their 3D representations of projects to be constructed. I took a step closer and found I was looking at a top-down view of Beenleigh.

I picked out the courthouse and the library. The model had all the streets marked out carefully and to scale. Worked into the streets and the buildings were carved runes which set it apart from the map I'd been using all day. The runes appeared to be some sort of Gaelic but for the life of me, I couldn't make sense of them. My eyes were drawn to a flashing red light at one end of the board.

The Old One moved toward it, leaning closer to the board as he studied the runes etched into that section.

I recognized the location: the Logan River Parklands, a sprawling park built along the twisting bends of the Logan River. It had plenty of exercise equipment and playgrounds for the kids. It was a common stop for parents and their children. Conor and Shay had loved it as youngsters.

It was also home to the local park run, not that I'd been in a year. Or three. I was going to have to remedy that if I took this bounty hunter gig seriously. I couldn't afford to be huffing and puffing from a stroll about the town. Maybe I'd head down there this weekend.

If you last that long.

"It's in the Parklands," Alasdair said. "On a weekday, plenty of people about. Another creature of Winter causing chaos?"

The Old One studied the glowing runes. "Crisp working, modest opening, short duration. Certainly Sidhe, but the location does make me wonder. Tread carefully, Alasdair, and take the rookie with you."

Rookie? It had never felt so good to be considered an amateur.

Alasdair grumbled, "Fine. Come on, comet," as he left the boardroom. "Let's see if we can't get you killed your first day on the job."

He left the boardroom and strode over to a bank of lockers, fiddled with a well-oiled padlock on one, and pulled it open. He took out a helmet and handed it to me.

"What's this for?" I asked, hoping my eagerness could dispel his gruff demeanor.

"Protection," Alasdair replied, shutting the locker.

I looked at the helmet and considered my encounter with the troll yesterday.

"This will really help protect me from the Sidhe?"

Alasdair gave me a look like he had sucked a lemon.

"No, from the road. Do try to hang on."

I felt like an idiot as he pushed open the back door and led the way to a large black and silver Harley-Davidson sitting behind the building. A second helmet waited for him on the seat.

He threw his leg over the bike, as I pulled the helmet down over my hair.

"What are you waiting for? An engraved invitation?" he asked.

I'd been trying to win him over with optimism and cheeriness, but if he was going to be an ass, in the hope he could drive me off, he would be bitterly disappointed.

I stepped into his space, right up against the bike.

"Alasdair, I get it. You don't want me here. You don't like having to drag a newbie around. Fair enough. Whether that's because I'm a woman or threw up the first time we met, I don't know. But what I do know is this—I need this job. Which means I need you. And as far as I can see from that empty room and wall full of coins, you're just about the last man standing. How long can that last?"

"What do you mean?" he asked, not moving an inch.

"Well, the other hunters are gone, aren't they?"

Sure, there was a chance there could be other hunters out roaming the town as we spoke, but that wasn't the vibe I got talking to Alasdair and the Old One. They were tired and worn out. The air in the Camp was thick with resignation. It felt like defeat that just hadn't happened yet.

I poked my finger into his chest. "Only a man could think that being the only bounty hunter in town is a good thing. You might as well paint a target on your back."

"What do you know about it?" he replied, his voice rising an octave.

"Only what you've told me. Which isn't a helluva lot," I said. "But if the Sidhe are half as wily as you seem to think, you've got to realize that if you're the only game in town, sooner or later they're going to start hunting you. The sooner they punch your ticket, the sooner they have free run of the place. I get the feeling the Old One doesn't hit the streets too often. Am I right?"

"He's retired from the field. Someone needs to run the Camp."

"Precisely. So unless you want every otherworldly creature in town coming for you, you need to recruit. Create a target-rich environment, so to speak. So stop moaning about my presence and get invested in my training. Because one of these days, they're going to come for you, and you're going to want someone watching your back."

Alasdair sat, silently considering my point, before nodding at the seat behind him. "Get on the bike."

I'll take that as a yes.

Men weren't particularly inclined to acknowledge when they were wrong, and I figured my gruff Scottish mentor was no exception. I swung my leg over the Harley and clambered on behind him. I looked around for somewhere to hold onto and realized there was nowhere else to put my arms but around him.

So, I wrapped them around his broad chest and found only muscle. Part of me was acutely aware of just how much of me was pressed up against his back, and just how good that felt.

Dammit, Nora, focus. This isn't the time to let your libido do the thinking for you.

Alasdair peeled out of the car park, sending a spray of gravel out behind the bike.

I hung on tight as we wound through town, rolling through the set of traffic lights at the top of City Road and down toward the Parklands at the edge of town. The road led to a round-about with an on-ramp to the freeway and another exit that I knew would take us to the park.

The question was, what was waiting for us there? What had caused that warning siren in the Camp?

Alasdair leaned to the left and my body followed his lead. We rounded a rocky plateau and the murky brown waters of the Logan River came into view. Alasdair slowed as we approached, scanning the vast green expanse before us.

The road through the Parklands itself ran in a large loop. It had been laid between the Logan River on the left and a small marsh surrounding an island on the right. The outer rim was where the play areas had been built, along with the walking trails and a few pontoon jetties leading down to the river.

Several narrow land bridges led through the reeds and marshes to a grassy mound that formed an island in the midst of the marsh. Sometimes local reenactment groups frequented the area, building forts and battling each other for control of the island. Today the area was vacant. The small gate leading to the causeway was locked.

Alasdair taxied into the car park. There were a dozen other vehicles, as well as a handful of families scattered about the play equipment.

A mother was walking a stroller along the outer circuit while another was doing her best to push two kids on the swings. A small fitness boot camp occupied a large grassy field.

There was no sign of an otherworldly presence anywhere.

Alasdair cut the engine and we climbed off the bike. He set his helmet down, raised his hand over the bike, and whispered something.

I felt a faint whiff of power that sent a tingle down my spine.

"What was that?" I asked.

"Just a little something to make sure the bike is still here when we get back. It wouldn't be the first time someone has tried to steal it."

Fair enough. This was Beenleigh, after all. It had something of a reputation for things disappearing when they were not bolted down. I imagined that the pristine Harley might be a tempting target for a thief or a teenager wanting a joyride.

"What will happen if they try?" I asked, my curiosity piqued.

Alasdair glanced at the seat of the bike. "The next person to sit on that seat without uttering the right counter-spell will feel like their ass is on fire for a week."

"Isn't that dangerous?" I asked.

"Only to them," Alasdair replied with a shrug. "In my experience, they don't make it more than about twenty feet before they decide to leg it. It's a teachable moment."

"You don't have any children, do you?"

"No," Alasdair replied. "Why?"

"Oh, it just shows in your teaching manner," I replied before realizing I probably shouldn't criticize my mentor to kick off our relationship.

Alasdair appeared unfazed. "Any complaints, take it up with the Old One. Rest assured that, next to the Old One, I'm a saint."

I thought back to meeting the Old One at his caravan. I could still recall the feel of the knife in my back.

I didn't doubt Alasdair for a minute.

"What do we do now?" I asked, hoping to change the subject.

"We keep our eyes open," he replied. He hadn't stopped scanning the park around us for any sign of trouble. "Just because we can't see it, doesn't mean it isn't here. The Sidhe are masters of deception, glamours, and veils. You can't trust your eyes when it comes to them."

"Then how will we know when we've found them?"

"Oh, you'll know," he replied cryptically. "Let's go. We won't find them here in the car park."

We started out of the car park, strolling along the footpath like a couple out for a late afternoon walk. Not that we held hands or anything. Something told me Alasdair wasn't interested enough in maintaining a cover to weather a public display of affection.

"The first thing you need to know about what we do, is the rules," Alasdair began.

I couldn't help but grin.

He took one sideways glance at my face and asked, "What are you smiling about?"

"You said *we*. I'm on the team," I replied with giddy excitement. It was far more than I'd expected when I set out this morning.

He shook his head. "You won't be for long unless you pay attention. Listen up."

"I'm listening. Hit me," I replied as my gaze followed the mother walking her pram. There wasn't anything unusual about her, but knowing the Sidhe were about gave me anxiety for her, and her baby.

"The first is that we are a part of society, not apart from society. Consider the consequences of your actions and those your actions expose to the supernatural world. Not everyone is cut out for handling it. You have some talent. I saw it in the library. Learn when to use it and when to hold it in reserve. The town trusts us because of the good work we've done. You take out a family as collateral damage, or vandalize town property, and that can turn everyone, including the authorities, against us. Got it?"

I nodded. "The good we do can't be outweighed by the damage we cause. Understood."

"That's one way to look at it," he replied. "The second is sacrifice. Hunters do what we do, so that others can have a better life, safe from the perils of the Otherworld, safe from the danger, stress, and trauma that we face every day. Embrace that sacrifice; use it to drive you. The path of the hunter is a lonely road. I know you are in it for the cash, but you have to understand it isn't all bounties and celebrations. The longer you do what we do, the more likely you are to mess up and when you do, you will get hurt. That is the price we pay, so others don't have to."

"Have you ever messed up?" I asked as we made our way around the circuit.

He pulled up the sleeve of his jacket. The flesh of his left arm above the wrist was dark and discolored. I'd never seen anything like it.

"Everyone makes mistakes. Rule three. Learn from them. You will live longer."

I reflected on the rules. "So, when it comes down to it—don't get caught, take a flogging for those who should never know about it, and don't get beaten the same way twice?"

"More or less," Alasdair replied.

We reached the end of the circuit and stood beneath the painted red bridge that spanned the Logan River.

We'd walked the length of the outer path and found nothing out of the ordinary.

"There's nothing here," I said. "Could the Camp's alarm system have malfunctioned?"

"If it can, I've never seen it," he said, turning away from the river to survey the marshes and the island on the other side of the ring road. "Which leaves us with that mess over there."

We set out toward the island, crossing the ring road and strolling down the grassy embankment toward the causeway. The island looked deserted, but as he walked, Alasdair's posture changed from casual stroll, to coiled and ready to strike, his hand never far from the machete in its sheath at the small of his back.

"Whatever you do, stay beside me or behind me where I can look out for you, and do exactly what I say. Now is not the time to be a smart ass, got it?"

I considered a quip, but I could read the room and thought better of it.

"Perfectly," I replied, wanting my reluctant mentor to know he could count on me.

A tingle started like a pinprick in my fingers, but after a few more steps, the hairs on the back of my neck stood on end. As we walked, the sensation grew stronger.

"Alasdair, can you feel that?" I whispered.

"Yes," he replied, pushing me behind him.

"What is it?" I asked.

"Sidhe magic," he said. "A lot of it."

We reached the island, but there was nothing except grass and trees as far as the eye could see.

Alasdair cleared his throat, loudly addressing the empty island.

"What's it going to be?" he called. "Are you going to skulk behind your glamours? Or are we going to talk?"

Only silence greeted him, and I wondered if I'd imagined the whole thing.

He raised a hand and whispered, *"Teine!"*

Flames rose from the palm of his hand until a broiling inferno roughly a foot high billowed from it.

"It looks like there isn't anyone here, Nora," he announced theatrically. "Guess we're okay to do a little back burning. These trees are looking out of control."

He strode toward the nearest tree, the white-hot flames above his hand wisping toward the bark.

"Stop!" A shrill voice cut through the warming air.

Alasdair closed his hand and the fires flickered out of existence. He had a smug look of satisfaction on his face.

Before us a shimmer rippled through the air, like an invisible curtain parting, and five beings appeared before us on the island.

Chapter 9

They were humanoid, but more slender and graceful. Their lithe curves made me a little self-conscious. Their fair skin was smooth and unblemished, and their eyes had a slight upward angular tilt to them.

Their leader had eyes that were unlike anything I'd ever seen: golden orbs set in white sclera with a long vertical slit for a pupil.

"You know better than to threaten a sanctuary, Alasdair," she said, staring down my new mentor.

"Well, well, well," Alasdair replied, "What brings you to my town, Naerine Oaksidhe?"

I stepped back, my jaw dropping open as the five warriors advanced.

Each of them wore armor of overlapping gold plates, held in place by leather straps and brass fittings. The clothes they wore beneath the armor were rich browns and greens that reminded me of an evergreen forest.

From the description and artistic depictions in the Otherworld journal, I surmised that these were Sidhe of the Summer Court. I tried not to smile. I didn't want to alarm them, but I was silently pleased with myself that my binge-reading was paying dividends. It also increased my confidence that the book itself was more a work of fact than fiction, in spite of the supernatural subject matter.

"It's been some time since the Summer Court paid us a visit," Alasdair prompted.

The Sidhe leader smiled, not the broad grin of someone enjoying themselves, but the forced smile of a politician enduring the presence of an unwelcome guest at a campaign event.

"Alasdair, you arrived swifter than I would have expected. Sitting on your hands today, are you? I would have expected you to be busier."

Alasdair took a step forward, raising both his hands. The calloused flesh spoke of hands used to doing manual labor. I'd also witnessed the power that could come out of them.

The Sidhe took a step back. Clearly, they were familiar with the pyromancer's gifts too.

"Oh, I have been extremely busy of late, but never too busy that I can't roll out the welcome wagon for our friends from the Summer Court."

Naerine raised an eyebrow. "Friends, are we? Do you say the same thing when we aren't present? I thought this was more a relationship of convenience, like a dog eating the scraps that fall from its master's table."

Alasdair bristled, rolling his shoulders as he took another step forward.

"Stop beating around the bush, Naerine. Tell me why you've set foot in my world, or we are going to have a diplomatic incident."

"We're tending to the sanctuary, Alasdair," Naerine replied, raising her hands and gesturing to the trees around her. "I have already said as much. Is your hearing going in your advanced years? How long does a human live nowadays? Decades shorter certainly, in your vocation, perhaps."

"I hear just fine," Alasdair replied, eying the Sidhe in turn. "Certainly enough to know when I am being fed a fallacy."

"You know better, Alasdair. The Sidhe cannot speak a lie," Naerine said, her voice melodious in spite of a complexion that was steadily growing more colored as she lost patience.

"You cannot speak a lie, but you are masters of obfuscation and omission. You have business beyond the sanctuary. Tell me why you're here or our day is going to get much worse."

Naerine placed a finger on Alasdair's chest, and I found myself chafing at her familiarity.

"Come now, Alasdair, we've done nothing, and under the Arcane Covenant we can pass through this realm providing we break neither your laws, nor those of the Congress. Now step aside. We have places to be."

Naerine turned to look at me and her nose wrinkled distastefully.

"I will do no such thing until you answer my question," Alasdair said, stepping right into Naerine's face. He was perilously close now; scant inches separated them. It was as if he had forgotten we were outnumbered five to two. Or perhaps he hadn't, and was simply trying to get close enough to their leader to make a move if need be.

If the Sidhe drew her weapon, a wicked-looking sword on her hip, Alasdair would have less than a second to react.

Trust him.

A trickle of sweat ran down my brow. No doubt Alasdair had been here before and knew what he was doing. I needed to watch and learn. That was why I was here. If what the Sidhe was saying was true, there was little Alasdair could do. Perhaps that was why Alasdair was seeking to provoke her. His aggressive stance would test both her resolve and her intentions. If the Sidhe took action against him, Alasdair could act in self-defense.

As he raised his hands, the sheath at the small of his back, beneath his jacket became more accessible. The handle on his machete protruded just far enough off his left hip that he could draw it swiftly.

"Enough, Alasdair. I won't play your game," Naerine replied. "Neither would I travel to this blighted wasteland if my mistress didn't demand it."

Her mistress? Titania was the Summer Queen. Was that who she was referring to? Or did Naerine serve one of the lesser nobles of the court?

"Wasteland is a bit harsh," I said, peering past Alasdair. "I know the town could use a little sprucing up, but wasteland feels unfair."

"Ignorance." Naerine scoffed, dismissing me as she pointed at Alasdair's face. "Step aside, Alasdair. Your arrogance is unearned. A human failing and a fleeting condition at that. Death is far more permanent. You can't hope to take us all, not on your best day."

"You might age well, Sidhe, but you bleed like everything else. Your mistress might be immortal but you sure as hell are not."

Naerine's hand went to her sword. "This is the last time I'm going to ask you to step aside. If you want trouble, I'll give it to you."

"We already have it," Alasdair replied. "You're in my town and are unwilling to tell me why. Level with me and you can be on your way."

The Sidhe let out an impatient sigh, like a parent accommodating a difficult child.

"If you must know, we are here investigating the increased trespassing of Winter in our domain. It can't have escaped your notice that a lieutenant of the Winter Court has been sighted in your city."

The sentence had an air of accusation about it.

"Perhaps you ought to be wasting his time rather than ours. Or are you afraid to face him?" she asked.

She had to be talking about the Redcap. Alasdair hesitated.

"If only that was the limit of things," Alasdair answered, backing down a little. "There have been others."

Naerine sniffed the air. "You do reek of Winter. I could smell you before I saw you."

Her golden eyes settled on me, and I felt intensely uncomfortable under her gaze. "And who is this you've brought with you?"

"Apprentice," Alasdair answered noncommittally. "Don't mind the smell. We put down an ice troll. You should know, troll guts just don't wash off easily."

"Ice troll?" Naerine's focus returned to Alasdair. "Where?"

He looked amused. "One of the Winter King's elite guards show up out of nowhere. Surely none of this is news to you?"

His words had a sarcastic edge to them. The Summer Sidhe had been baiting him with the Red Cap, but he'd turned the tables on them.

Naerine looked at the other Sidhe. "The situation is worse than we believed. Winter grows increasingly bold."

Alasdair scratched at his beard. "I know. You've been dropping the ball, but don't worry, we've taken care of things on that front. We took out the ice troll ourselves, so no need to worry yourselves on his account."

"Well, that explains your unusual sense of bravado," Naerine answered with a laugh. "You killed a brainless thug and now you think you're invincible."

"I'm in good form for an old man," Alasdair replied. "Test me and see. I dare you."

"Another time, perhaps," Naerine replied. "I wouldn't want to leave your apprentice without a master. You can stand down, Alasdair. Clearly our interests are aligned. Winter is here, not by accident but by intention. They are looking for something and it's in our best interests to find it first. Do you have any idea what it might be?"

Alasdair shrugged. "I'm afraid I didn't stop to ask the troll any questions. I cut off his head as quickly as I could and was done with him."

"Well, none of us will mourn his passing," Naerine replied, "but we're no closer to understanding why they're here. If you'll excuse us, we have work to do."

"Give me your word that you are not here to harm my people and I will let you pass."

Alasdair extended his hand, palm open, ready to shake.

Bargains, the language of the Sidhe. Once they entered into one, they could not break it, no matter how they might want to. The journal's warning had been clear though. One did need to always act with caution when treating with the Sidhe. They were wily and cunning enough to keep the letter while breaking the spirit of their agreements. Perhaps that was why Alasdair had been so broad and all-encompassing with his bargain.

Naerine grasped Alasdair's outstretched hand and shook it. "I swear, I have no intention of harming you or any of the humans of this good town. I do however intend great harm to the forces of Winter that have trespassed in our domain."

Alasdair shook Naerine's hand. "Then we have an accord."

"But Alasdair," Naerine added, not letting go of his hand, "should you get in our way, I can give you no such assurance. Those who stand against the light of Summer will wilt before her majesty."

I stared at the strange pair.

"If you go about town like that, you're going to cause a stir," I muttered. Hell, there were parts of Beenleigh where a shirt and thongs was considered overdressed. The five heavily-armored Sidhe were far from discreet.

"Don't trouble yourself, dear." Naerine cocked her head at Alasdair. "A little long in the tooth to be starting a new career, isn't she?"

Long in the tooth? How dare she? I tried to contain the urge to punch her in her perfect face as Alasdair shuffled between me and Naerine.

"She helped with the troll," he replied. "How many ice trolls have you killed, Naerine?"

It was about the closest thing to a compliment Alasdair had given me, and I beamed with pride.

"More than you," she answered, looking at the back of her manicured finger nails as she troubled a speck of dirt caught there. "By a considerable margin, I would expect. And I didn't need help to do it."

Alasdair shook that one off. "What the Old One wants, the Old One gets. You ought to know that."

Naerine recoiled a little. "What interest does the pond dweller have in her?"

Alasdair shook his head. "Damned if I know, but he seems to have taken a liking to her, so a bounty hunter she'll be, until she gets herself killed."

Naerine looked at me, her gold eyes boring into mine as if she were trying to read my soul.

"Consider this your first lesson," she said, as she clicked her fingers. Her armor vanished. Her alien features were gone, and a human woman stood before us, her golden hair pulled back in a neat ponytail. The only sign of Naerine was the luminous golden eyes. "This ought to do, don't you think?"

How the hell had she done that?

She adjusted the neat pantsuit she was wearing, before rapping her fist against the front of her outfit. There was a clang of her fist striking steel, and she smiled.

"It's a glamour. The Sidhe know how to move about discreetly when we must. We've been visiting this world since the dawn of time."

The other Sidhe affected similar glamours. Alasdair stood aside, letting the five of them march over the causeway, where they hopped into a maxi-taxi that was idling there. It pulled out onto the ring road, leaving us alone on the island.

"I really do hate the Sidhe," Alasdair grumbled, "but of all the arrogant ass hats in the Otherworld, I think I dislike Naerine the most."

The two of them clearly had history. From where and when, I could only guess.

"Not the first time you two have met, then?" I probed.

"Unfortunately not," he replied, as he started walking back to his bike. "She puts on a show, but do not be deceived. If the Queen told her to slit your throat, she would do it in a heartbeat. The Summer Sidhe might be less malevolent and cruel in their interactions with mortals, but they will absolutely kill you if you get in their way."

"So why did you let them pass?" I asked, a little confused.

"Like she said, they are afforded certain protections under the agreements that bind our respective nations. There are laws governing how the civilized elements of the supernatural world are to behave. Taking up arms against them without provocation would bring us all sorts of strife. The Congress might have little sway here, largely because they ignore us, but rest assured, if the Sidhe brought them a complaint, they would show up here in a heartbeat and make their displeasure known. Fear the day you meet the Congress, or any of its lickspittles."

Well, that was a pleasant thought. I would have to read up on the Congress. I hadn't come across any reference to it in the Otherworld journal, but if it was the government of the wizarding world here in the mortal realm, that would explain its absence. Perhaps my mother would know more about it. My father had been gifted. Maybe he'd had dealings with them.

Following Alasdair as he made a beeline for his bike, I changed the topic.

"So how do we go about getting paid?" I asked.

Alasdair turned, his brow furrowing. "For what exactly?"

"For this? Working?" I replied, wondering why I needed to explain the notion to him. If he made ten grand for the ice troll, I was curious how much money he made on days like today.

"For talking to the Sidhe?" he asked as we reached the bike.

"Yeah, for this sort of thing." I lifted my helmet off the seat.

"It's not a bounty, so nothing."

"Wait? What?" I stammered.

Alasdair chuckled. "Consider this the groundwork to getting paid. Until one of those pointy-eared nuisances steps out of line, we are simply pounding the pavement. We take down something on the board, or some supernatural creature shows up, causing mischief and we end it, then we get paid. It's not exactly consistent, but it can be considerable."

"So we're not getting paid for today?" I asked, trying to keep the disappointment out of my voice and failing miserably.

"No," he replied, as he reversed his earlier incantation. "That's the life, though. Feast one day, famine the next. Really makes you wonder why you want to do this in the first place."

I could see what he was doing, trying to discourage me from becoming a hunter, but clearly, he didn't understand how dire my money situation was.

Besides, these were two of the most interesting days I'd had in my life. I'd survived the troll, met the Old One, and encountered a handful of Summer Sidhe.

And if what I'd read in the Otherworld was any indication, I'd barely scratched the surface of the wonders the supernatural world contained. Now that my eyes were open, I couldn't pretend it didn't exist anymore.

I swung my leg over the bike as he fired up the engine. "You're not getting rid of me that easily."

"I won't have to," Alasdair replied. "With Summer and Winter flocking to the city like this, we'll be lucky to survive the week."

Chapter 10

Alasdair pulled up in front of my home, and I climbed off the motorbike. Turning, I found my reluctant mentor staring at me.

"What?" I asked, shifting from one foot to the other. The focus of his hard brown eyes made me nervous.

"If you hear anything I say today, I want you to hear this." His gaze drifted to the yard where my mother, Bran, and Conor were playing. "You have a nice life here, Nora. Money isn't everything."

"Spoken like someone who has plenty of it," I replied. "I need this, Alasdair. They need this. I'll see you tomorrow."

"So I'm not gonna be able to talk you out of this, then?"

The bike idled, a slow quiet rumble that filled the silence as he waited for my answer.

"I don't think so." I shook my head gently. "I have to be able to take care of my family."

"What if I paid your rent for you?" he asked. "Bought you a little breathing room until the library reopens."

I stopped dead. Had he really just said that? Offered to cover my rent? He hardly even knew me.

The memory of the troll rampaging through the library flooded my mind and brought with it a surge of the terror I had felt there. The notion of hunting creatures from the Otherworld scared the crap out of me. Part of me wanted to take him up on the offer. But another part of me, the part of me that had relied on a man for the better part of two decades, the part of me that was desperate to be independent again, couldn't accept that kind of charity.

Besides, I knew too much now; had seen too much. Rampaging trolls and the Sidhe courts. There was simply no unknowing these things.

"I can't do that," I replied, putting my hands on my hips. "I can't take your charity, but I can do this. I just need someone to teach me."

"It's not charity." Alasdair sighed. "If it helps, think of it as your share from the troll kill. You said it yourself. You helped. You deserve a little something. Take the money, pay your rent, and live a better life than this."

There was a loneliness in his words that I hadn't sensed earlier. Was that why he was so intent on warning me away? I was conflicted inside. Everything he was saying seemed genuine, but in my experience, men tended to be sweet until they got what they wanted and then they traded you in for a legal secretary.

I didn't know if I could trust Alasdair. Perhaps he liked being the only hunter in town. It certainly gave him free pick of the bounties coming through the Camp.

"Why would you do that?" I asked, a little skeptical, but I didn't let it show in my tone. "When I suggested it in the library, you laughed at me. Now you want to give me the money. Have you gone soft on me, old man?"

There was a mischievous twinkle in the corner of Alasdair's eye as he smiled. "Or maybe you've proved to be such a persistent pain in the ass that I want to get rid of you before you get me killed."

That wasn't it. At least I was fairly sure it was something else. Perhaps he wasn't being honest with himself either.

"You're going to have to do better than that," I replied.

He let out a pained groan. "You aren't one of us, Nora, not yet. Not till you take your first bounty. You could take the cash now and walk away, free from the danger that comes with this life. If you become a hunter, you invite the Otherworld into your life, into your home. It will find its way here eventually. It always does."

There was a sadness in his voice, a tangible pain on the tip of his tongue.

I stood there quietly. I didn't know what to say to that.

Alasdair's gaze never wavered. It was like he could feel my hesitation.

"Look, just think on it, okay?" he said. "And if you see reason, I'll give you the cash. Otherwise, I guess I'll see you tomorrow."

I nodded. "I'll see you tomorrow, Alasdair."

He shook his head and muttered something about women, but it was lost in the rev of the Harley's huge engine. He took off up the street. I couldn't help but wonder what it would feel like to have those big arms wrapped around me. I'd had mine around him for the better part of the last half-hour. There was more muscle than I'd expected, hidden beneath that leather coat.

"Get a grip," I told myself. Damn these hormones always pushing me toward poor decisions. I didn't need another Judas. I certainly didn't need to complicate things with my mentor any more than they already were.

I couldn't afford that kind of distraction right now. I let out a resigned sigh as he disappeared around the corner.

Once he'd gone, I made my way up the side of the house and let myself through the side fence. Bran bounded over to me, as Conor looked up from my mother's lap.

"Mum!" he called. The eagerness in his voice seemed to drive away the day's worry. It felt good to have someone who was always excited to see me.

"There's my boy," I said. "How was your day with Gran?"

"Oh, we had a world of fun, didn't we?" my mother answered, wrapping her arm around him to keep him hostage.

Conor giggled that little laugh of his, and I plopped down beside them. The screen door opened, and Shay emerged carrying a jug of water, a stack of plastic cups, and a bag of chips. I'd caught them in the middle of their afternoon snack. No wonder they always ate less dinner when Gran watched them.

"Hey Mum, you're home early," she said as she looked for somewhere to stash the chips.

I waved her over. I hadn't told the kids about the library, and I didn't want to worry them. They had enough going on in their lives without fretting about money at home. Conor, particularly. He didn't do well with stress.

"Sure am, honey. Is one of those for me?" I asked, pointing at the cups. I was parched. A drink stop hadn't really ranked high on Alasdair's to-do list.

"Of course." Shay set the cups and the chips on the lawn, but the cups fell over. The grass in the backyard was a little longer than it should have been. With all the rain over the summer, it had grown like weeds, and I was fairly sure there were a few of those mixed in, too.

My mother grabbed the cups and separated them, before nestling each down into the grass so that it wouldn't topple over.

Conor grabbed the chips and pressed the sides of the packet until the top split open with a loud pop. He laughed uncontrollably.

"So what are we all doing out here?" I asked. I'd expected to find Conor on his computer, playing with his friends.

"Some of the boys from Conor's class last year were giving him a hard time online," Shay whispered to me, "so we brought him out to play with Bran. He always seems to cheer Conor up."

The big Irish wolfhound nuzzled against Conor while trying to get his nose into the bag of chips.

"No chips for you," Conor said, pointing at the dog bowl. It was filled to overflowing. "You've already had your treats."

That didn't dissuade Bran at all as he playfully tussled with Conor.

"Bullies," my mother whispered, her voice soft, but hard. I knew that tone; it was the calm at the center of a hurricane.

Things were quiet, quieter than you expected until all hell broke loose.

"Why do kids have to be so cruel?" she asked. "When will they learn that different is good?"

I let out a sigh. This wasn't the first time Conor had run into trouble at school. Back in the third grade, we'd had a lot of trouble with a bully named Brian. It had gone on for weeks until Conor refused to go to school. I tried working with teachers, tried contacting the boy's parents. None of it had worked. Then Shay had caught the little punk pushing her brother around. She'd shoved Brian so hard, he'd tripped over the chain bordering the footpath and landed in the garden.

If her teacher's account of the confrontation was accurate, she had threatened him in no uncertain terms what she might do to him should he ever raise a hand to her brother again.

It had worked, at least for a time. I should have been grateful for that. We'd had enough support from the teacher aides to keep him at the same school as his sister. Conor was quite bright; it was just his condition that made schooling difficult.

I wrapped my arm around him and pulled him close to me.

"We'll take care of it," I replied, speaking largely to Shay and my mother. "I'll be damned if I let some little punk chase my boy out of school."

"So how was your day?" my mother asked. "Find anything interesting? Other than that big hunk of a man who bought you home?"

"Mum," I warned.

"What? I'm old, not blind. Or dead, for that matter. He could take me for a ride any time."

"Mum, the kids," I said.

"On his bike, of course," my mother replied, waving off my protestations. "They'll learn about these things, sooner or later, my dear. Best they learn about them here, trust me."

I was too tired to argue but certainly not up for an impromptu sex-ed lesson either.

"His name is Alasdair," I began. "I ran into him at one of the businesses I visited. He was kind enough to give me a lift home."

"Definitely an improvement on the last little weasel you dated," my mother replied with a shrug. "Maybe you should have invited him in."

"Mum," I hissed. I tried not to bad-mouth Judas in front of the kids. They could form their own opinion. "They don't need to hear this."

I cocked my head at the kids.

She smiled at my discomfort, which was infuriating, but her wry grin did make it difficult to stay angry at her for long.

"Best damn thing he ever did, bringing these little angels into the world."

She wasn't wrong. Whatever differences I might have with Judas, and as miserable as my marriage had become, the union was responsible for Shay and Conor. For that, I was grateful every day.

"Have you heard anything from my father recently?" I asked. I didn't know what possessed me, but I thought perhaps I might catch her off-guard while she was distracted.

Her features sharpened, her smile fading as she turned on me.

"Now why would you ruin a perfectly good afternoon by asking about that egomaniac? He and Judas are cut from the same cloth, always working, ego the size of Uluru, and that's all I have to say about it."

There was an air of finality to her tone. It didn't settle things in my mind. I'd never met the man, and part of me always wondered what he was like. I must have gotten my talents from him. What kind of wizard was he?

At least my children knew their father. How much input he was going to have in their lives from here on out, though, was a matter for the courts to decide. The one perk of his young, limber new girlfriend was that she seemed to keep him distracted. I was both grateful and infuriated at the same time. Which I could be; as a woman, that was my right.

"I guess, as I look back at everything that is happening to me," I said, "I just wonder what the catalyst was for the two of you splitting?"

"He was a slave to his job," my mother replied. "He seldom had time for me. As a foolish young woman, I found his confidence and status alluring. But the longer I spent in his ivory tower, the more I realized the work addiction was an incurable disease that would consume him. We didn't split amicably, dearie. I left one summer's morning and ran like my life depended on it. You don't know the kinds of things your father is capable of, but I do. If I have any say in it, you never will."

Draining my cup of water in three big gulps, I set it down. Well, that was something. Not exactly what I'd hoped for, but at least it was something.

I reached into the bag of corn chips, pulled out two of the salted triangular slices of heaven, and popped them in my mouth. They broke with a satisfying crunch as I bit through them and realized just how hungry the day's adventure had left me.

"Well," I said, rising to my feet, "enough of that for one day, I think. Come on, everybody, inside. Time for tea."

I shepherded my mother and the kids across the patio to the back door only to find a line of fine white granules laid purposefully across the doormat. The line stretched from one side of the door to the other.

"What's all this, then?" I pointed at the line. It looked like an entire container of perfectly good salt on the ground. "This is how you get ants."

"Don't look at me," Shay replied, stepping over it and into the house. "It was Gran."

"It'll keep the Fae out," Conor replied with a big grin.

I should have assumed as much. I shook my head and stepped over the threshold as I wondered if there was any truth in the old myth. I had not come across anything about it in the Otherworld journal, but I supposed if one had cold iron to hand, salt seemed more of a joke than a deterrent.

I thought of the troll rampaging through the library, and Alasdair's warning about joining the Camp. For the first time, my mother's paranoia was more comforting than bothersome. I'd do anything to keep them all safe.

"I fixed a stew for dinner," my mother said. "I wasn't sure what you had planned."

She was giving me far too much credit. I hadn't planned a meal in weeks. My current meal preparation could more accurately be described as winging things with whatever I could find in my fridge.

"Sounds great," I said, relieved to have one less chore to contend with.

"You know," she continued, "I don't have much going on this week. I was thinking I might stay here, help you with the kids and the house. At least until they go back to school next week."

"I don't want to go back to school," Conor replied, his eyes glistening. I knew the bullies were weighing on his mind.

"Don't worry, buddy, we'll take care of everything. Let's enjoy the rest of the holidays first."

Conor didn't seem wholly convinced, but he made his way over to the dinner table and planted himself on his chair. The same one as always, the one on my left.

We polished off Mom's stew, a hearty chicken and potato concoction that warmed me from the inside out. As soon as the bowls were empty, I shuffled the kids off to the showers while Mom tackled the dishes.

"Thanks for all the help." I picked up the last of the empty bowls from the table and carried them to the dishwasher.

"Don't mention it," she said. "Happy to help where I can, but you need to pull yourself together, dear. The children will start noticing soon."

Love with a dash of disappointment, that was my mom. Or perhaps that was just my inner critic making things into more than they were. She was worried. Perhaps because she'd been where I was, and I had two children to care for, not just the one like she had.

"I'm going to head upstairs and get some rest," I said, popping the dish soap in the dishwasher before closing the door and turning it on.

My mother nodded. "You might not think much about the Otherworld, dear, but a troll—"

"Mum," I interrupted, not ready for a lecture.

"It's high time we took some action to secure this house," she said, ignoring my pleading look. "You've never had it warded. There's little, if any, iron about, and a determined Sidhe of negligible talent would be in here in a heartbeat."

I wasn't ready to argue with my mother. The memory of the ice troll and the image of the Red Cap on the bounty board was playing heavily on my mind.

"Tell you what, why don't you have a think about what we should do first, and tomorrow we'll set about taking care of it?" I replied, hoping to save myself the rest of her tirade.

My mother stood, her hands planted on her hips, a gesture I'd inherited from her. The sudden shift in my opinion on the Otherworld and her obsessive paranoia concerning it seemed to have taken her by surprise. Was she going to question my sudden change in attitude, or was she going to let me sleep? I prayed that it would be the latter.

She nodded. "Very good. I'm glad to see this business at work is starting to open your eyes."

It wasn't the whole truth. The real reason for indulging her was Alasdair's warning. It echoed the words of the Otherworld journal and frankly, it scared the hell out of me.

At a minimum, I knew there were five summer Sidhe running around town. Not to mention the Red Cap and his insane bounty. Any measures I could take to protect my family seemed both prudent and timely.

I headed upstairs and locked myself in my room, then grabbed the Otherworld journal from where I'd left it by my pillow.

What was it that Alasdair and the Old One had said? I wasn't a bounty hunter until I worked my first bounty. In my mind's eye, I could see the bounty board at the Camp. Six beings occupied it, from the Red Cap to the nameless pixie vandalizing my kid's school. They were the answer to all my problems. They would pay the rent. They would get me the money I needed to take care of my family.

I'd read *The Art of War*, and Sun Tzu said it better than anyone else.

If you know the enemy and know yourself, you need not fear the result of a hundred battles. If you know yourself but not the enemy, for every victory gained you will also suffer a defeat. If you know neither the enemy nor yourself, you will succumb in every battle.

I had six enemies, none of them from this world. I opened the journal and set it down at my desk.

There was research to be done.

Chapter 11

I pondered on the wisdom of my current course as I drove through Beenleigh.

The Old One and Alasdair had been crystal clear. If I wanted to be a hunter, I needed to take a bounty. I figured it was the only way they would stop trying to discourage me and actually become invested in my training.

Because if everything I'd read in the Otherworld journal, and everything Alasdair had told me, was correct, that was how I got off neutral ground and into the game. A deadly game, but one that could actually provide the kind of livelihood my kids deserved.

It was dangerous, but so what? I could die in a car accident tomorrow. Fate didn't care whether I was a librarian or a bounty hunter. She'd come for me anyway.

What I needed was a target. I had memorized the bounty board. While I wasn't nearly arrogant or stupid enough to tackle the Red Cap, there was a creature on the board that seemed a little more my speed. A more fitting target for an aspiring bounty hunter: the pixie vandalizing the local high school.

According to the Otherworld journal, pixies were the bottom of the food chain, more mischievous than dangerous and with a short attention span. That I could handle. At least with some help from the journal.

I considered asking Alasdair for help, but I couldn't be sure he would give it to me. The Old One had needed to compel him to take me along the day before. He hadn't even told me what time to show up today. I guess he figured I wouldn't bother.

I wasn't in the habit of letting men tell me what to do or when to do it. I'd had enough of that during my marriage. With Judas' exit from my life, I determined that I wouldn't allow anyone else to appoint themselves to the role.

Pulling into the school car park, I found it mostly deserted, probably due to the fact that it was still the holidays. A couple of cars were parked close to the administration building. The principal's car was there; an old Ford pulled in nose-first in a space labeled for his use. The beat-up old car had certainly seen better days, but it had recently been washed.

I did a lap of the car park and then backed into a space not too far from Principal Dare's. After all, he was the one who had placed the bounty on the pixie, and I thought it best to swing by his office. I couldn't just go sneaking around the school without his leave.

I'd met Principal Dare a number of times over the years as we explored how we could best cater to Conor's special skills. He'd always been accommodating and kind, yet stern as you'd expect from someone in his position.

I got out of the car, made my way to the boot, and took out a shoulder slung duffel bag.

While I'd never met a pixie, I felt a little more comfortable about facing my foe after reading the Otherworld journal. I knew I could expect it to be wickedly fast. They had to be, on account of being the bottom rung of the Fae pecking order. But the author had also noted that they suffered from a terrible attention span which contributed to an inability to process complex instructions.

If possible, I wanted to avoid killing the creature. After all, it hadn't done anything to me. The bounty only mentioned that the school wanted to be rid of it. So, I planned to capture it and take it to the Camp as proof that I had taken my first bounty.

Slinging the duffel bag over my shoulder, I closed the boot and locked it behind me. There might not be many kids around, but the last thing I needed was for my car to be taken for a joyride.

The old five-fingered discount ran rife in this area.

It was a nice day to be outside. The morning sun was warming gently, not the oppressive heat we'd had yesterday. The groundskeeper had already done his rounds and the scent of freshly cut grass wafted through the school. I headed straight for the administration building, a single floor, old brick building that had recently had a fresh coat of paint applied.

For my bounty hunting, I'd chosen jeans and an old motorcycle jacket I'd found in the garage. It was pretty worn and a little warm for the weather, but I figured a layer of protection couldn't hurt.

Pushing open the door, I stepped inside and was greeted by Janine. She was a good deal younger than me, bubbly and friendly. Which I might have found more endearing if she wasn't effortlessly slim in spite of her sedentary job. Clearly, she found more time to exercise than I did, or was blessed with good genes. I'd heard of them; they belonged to other people. I supposed I had my mother to thank for that—and my weakness for milk chocolate that was wildly at odds with my exercise regime. And by regime, I meant that whenever I felt like exercising I lay down until the feeling went away.

"Can I help you?" Janine asked, looking up from her keyboard.

"You certainly can. I'm here to see Principal Dare," I said, easing the duffel onto the counter to relieve myself of its weight.

Janine eyed the beaten-up duffel that had been stuffed to the brim and then scrutinized me again, scrunching up her face.

"He doesn't appear to have any appointments in his schedule. Can I ask you for your name?"

"Nora Byrne. He's not expecting me, but I'm here in response to his request for assistance. Tell him I'm from the Camp. He'll understand."

She raised an eyebrow, but slid back her rolling office chair, stood, and guided me around the corner to the principal's office. Principal Dare smiled as he looked up from a stack of paperwork.

"Nora, please, come in."

I closed the door behind me, mainly to keep his overeager receptionist from eavesdropping on our conversation. Principal Dare might be privy to the fact that I was working for the Camp, but I didn't want the rest of the school gossiping about what that might entail. I had enough trouble without anyone getting wind of what I was doing, let alone Judas. He'd surely use it for leverage against me in court.

Principal Dare was a man in his early fifties, with a balding pate and a round belly that hung over his belt. He had a kind smile and bushy eyebrows that were growing out of control.

"I must say, I wasn't expecting you," he began, running his hand along the edge of his desk. "When I placed the bounty, your boss accepted it, but told me it was unlikely they would be able to assist. Something about other, more pressing threats."

"Well, an opportunity presented itself, and I know you're back to school shortly. The last thing I want is that little creature causing problems for the students. My children included."

Principal Dare nodded. It wouldn't hurt for him to think he'd received preferential treatment.

"Nora, I thought you worked at the library. Frankly you are the last person I'd have expected to show up here. On account of your—"

"Principal Dare." I didn't want him to finish that train of thought. It had taken me all night to muster the courage to do this. I didn't need someone casting doubt on me now.

"Call me Arthur, please."

"Arthur, if you're going to say something about my age, or the fact that I'm a woman, I swear, I'll walk out that door and leave you to deal with the pixie on your own. Let's see what the parents say when their children come back after the break and find a creature from the Otherworld has taken up residence here."

There was doubt in his expression. He didn't think I could do it. I could almost hear his thoughts. How was I, an overweight woman in her forties, going to do a thing about the pixie that had caused him no end of trouble?

I didn't know whether the words were his or just my inner critic, but I could sense his judgment.

"It's not that at all," he replied. "You have always been so kind. I'd have thought you were the last one to go for this sort of thing."

"I go where the work takes me," I replied, not apologizing for my assumptions or for putting words in his mouth. He might have said otherwise, but Arthur Dare was a man skilled at handling others. He wasn't fooling me for a minute.

"If it's all the same with you, we are quite under the hammer at the moment, so if you'll point me toward your pixie problem, I'll take care of it and be on my way."

"Of course, of course." He nodded, massaging a welt on the back of his right hand. "Nasty little blighter it is, too. Only this morning I went to see if it was still holed up in our home economics kitchen. He tried to shiv me with a broken razor blade before flying off."

"It's in the kitchen?" I asked.

"He's barricaded himself in the walk-in pantry and won't come out. I suspect he's been stuffing himself on the ingredients there."

"Probably," I said. "Pixies do love a good feed."

I'd tucked a bag of gobstoppers into my bag for just that reason. I was hoping I could bait the pixie out and bargain with it. He was a fairy after all, and there was no reason I couldn't negotiate with him. I tried not to think about the fact

I was an adult offering a tiny creature candy to get in my car, but I didn't see any other way to get him out without doing him harm.

"Well, I know the way," I said. "Do you have a key I can use if things are locked?"

"Sure." Arthur reached for his keys and slipped one off the ring. "Here's my master key. It'll get you into just about any door on the grounds. I'll need it back, though."

"No worries, I'll bring you the pixie and your key as soon as I can." I took the key from his outstretched hand and pocketed it.

"Do take care, Nora. He's a murderous little rascal. He may not be large but he's scrappy."

"Rest assured, I've seen worse," I replied. "Two days ago, I fought an ice troll. How difficult can a pixie be?"

I let that question linger for him as I lifted my duffel and headed for the door. The surprise on his face was priceless.

"I do have someone coming by, so when you're done, just drop the key at the front desk with Janine. I've already put the bounty in escrow. It will be released to the Camp as soon as the creature is dealt with."

I couldn't help but think it might be an excuse for Arthur to save face. He seemed eager to avoid another face-to-face with his miniature nemesis.

"Consider it handled," I replied, before shutting the door behind me.

I waved at Janine as I breezed past her, heading for the kitchens. They were located next to the oval. The students used it to cater for functions, but most often it was used for sausage sizzles at Saturday sport.

I picked up my pace, not because I thought the creature might escape but because I thought the effort was good for my lungs. I wasn't going to get any fitter by imagining it. Power of positive thinking hadn't done anything for my stamina the last twenty years. There was no reason to believe it would start now.

Reaching the kitchens, I slipped my key into the lock and paused. Was I really ready for this?

I made my way into the large, commercial-looking kitchen. There were six standing benches for food preparation along each side of the room. Each had its own sink, stove-top, and utensils. In one corner of the room was a large storeroom and beside it a handful of fridges. A door down the far end led out of the kitchen and into a classroom.

The kitchen was quiet, far quieter than I had expected. I looked about for any sign of the pixie but found none. Setting my duffel bag on a bench, I reached into it and pulled out the bag of gobstoppers. There was enough sugar to last the little creature days. I peeled open the packet, loudly and intentionally, hoping the creature would overhear.

Pixies were known as the little ones by those who believed in the Otherworld. And while I didn't know its name, I thought there was a chance it might answer the call.

"Oh, little one? I brought you a treat I thought you might like."

I'd never negotiated with a pixie, but I did have two children and if there was one thing I'd learned, it was the value of a well-executed bribe.

When it had been time for Shay's toilet training, lollies had saved us from dozens of 'accidents'. Conor still did his homework because it was a prerequisite for dessert.

I opened the box and shook it. The large round gobstoppers clinked together in a satisfying way. I hoped my sweet currency would work on the mischievous pixie.

There was a shuffle in the pantry and my gaze locked onto the doors. The expansive walk-in pantry was where all the catering ingredients were stored. Beside it was a bank of fridges. While the door leading into the pantry was deceptively small, I knew the room itself was at least three meters square. Plenty of places for such a diminutive creature to hide and enough food to endure a siege.

"I guess I'll have to eat all of these sweets myself then." I hefted one of the gobstoppers and held it up like a precious gem.

The door to the pantry cracked open an inch, and a tiny voice called out, "A treat for me? Why?"

Its voice had a high pitch to it, but dragged the last syllable in each sentence.

"I was hoping we could make a deal," I replied, emboldened by his response.

"What kind of deal?" The pixie's voice dropped an octave, as he regarded me with one eye through the slender crack in the door. "How do I know the fat one hasn't sent you to trick me?"

The pixie had all the skepticism of a child speaking to one of its parents who had broken their promise, one too many times.

"Because I have the lollies here, don't I?" I crouched, so I was down at his height. "I can give them to you. You can check them for yourself."

I held one up to my mouth as if I were about to pop it inside. "I assure you they are delicious. But if you don't want them, I am more than happy to eat them myself."

"Wait, no!" The pixie pushed open the door and took a few tentative steps toward me, waving his little hand. Then he stopped and looked around, realizing that he'd left the safety of the pantry.

He was an odd-looking little guy, with purple skin and tufts of blue hair that were sticking out from underneath the measuring cup he was using as an improvised helmet. His outfit appeared to be a bag of Skittles that he'd cut holes in for his arms and legs. He was small enough he could sit comfortably on the palm of my hand.

So much trouble in such a small package.

The Skittles bag was held in place by a rubber band, and tucked into the side of it like a sword was half of a razor blade. Hardly a deadly weapon, but if Principal Dare's experience was any indication, he was more than willing to use it. The

Little Ones also knew some magic, so I erred on the side of caution.

I held out the candy.

The pixie eyed it warily. Then he grabbed it with a lightning-quick motion that I almost missed. One moment the gobstopper was in my hand; the next it was on the way to his mouth. I wondered how he would approach it. After all, it was almost half the size of his head.

"Now they're meant to last a while. So you'll want to lick it first," I said.

With the disobedience of a three-year-old child, the pixie popped the gobstopper between his teeth and bit down hard.

Unfortunately, they were called gobstoppers for a reason. The pixie nearly broke his teeth before the lolly shot out of his mouth. He caught it deftly in his hand, as his cheeks darkened.

"Nasty old hag tricked me," he shouted before hurling the lolly at the floor. It struck the linoleum and shattered into a dozen pieces. "Tried to break Sleet's teeth."

That had to be his name. Sleet.

Drawing his little sword, he launched himself through the air at me. With two beats of his wings, he was upon me and brandishing the blade. I shielded my face with my hands and was rewarded with a wicked slice that drew blood on my left palm.

"You nasty little—" I bit off the words before I let them out of my mouth. Neither of my children had ever attempted to shank me with a broken razor blade, so I was on unfamiliar ground.

The creature darted about my head, wings beating, hacking and slashing with the little dagger.

"Fat lady tries to trick me, but Sleet's not stupid."

I retreated to the bench, trying to fend him off with one hand, while reaching into my duffel.

I pulled out a rolled-up newspaper with a rubber band around it and turned to face my tiny foe. The pixie hurtled toward me, blade raised. Channeling my memories of Year Nine softball, I swung as hard as I could.

Rolled up paper met Sleet midair and sent him cartwheeling through the room before he landed with a thud on the linoleum floor. He skidded until he came to a halt. He rose to his feet, took one look at me, and darted back into the pantry, slamming the door behind him.

"Go away," he shouted. "That's your last warning."

I looked at the shattered lolly and sighed. Clearly, I'd had the right idea, but the wrong bait. The journal had said pixies had a wicked appetite, but my diminutive friend had clearly met his match with the hard lolly.

I had half a dozen stinging red cuts where he'd broken my skin. It was certainly a good thing I had come after the pixie and not the Red Cap. He wouldn't have left me in one piece.

Unwilling to quit, and frankly a little embarrassed at how much damage the pixie had down with a broken box-cutter's blade, I paused to reconsider the situation.

The principal, Alasdair, the Old One, all of them; they all thought I should head on back to the library and take whatever life decided to give me. Perhaps they were all right.

Maybe I was too old for this. A bloody pixie, the least of all the dangers of the Otherworld, was running circles around me.

I shook my head. I wasn't going to let one bad-mouthed little fairy get the best of me. Not today. Too much was riding on this. I reached into my duffel, pulled out a small first-aid kit, and patched the wounds.

Not that I was in any danger of bleeding out, but it gave me something to do while I thought of a better plan. Looking around the kitchen, I noticed a few ingredients laying around. A bag of flour here, some sugar there. One of the fridges had a packet of chocolate chips waiting to be used.

I gathered the ingredients together, pulled out a mixing bowl, and went to work. If a gobstopper wouldn't do the trick, I knew something that might. Perhaps I'd just tried the wrong bribe.

Mom's choc-chip cookie recipe. Guaranteed to smell extraordinary and taste even better. The warm crumbly cookies simply melted in your mouth. I'd made them so many times I didn't even need a recipe.

I pulled out a set of measuring cups, a mixing bowl, and a baking tray. Finding some butter in the fridge and a little greaseproof paper, I worked it over the tray so the cookies wouldn't stick and preheated the oven to a toasty one-eighty degrees Celsius.

I talked as I worked, knowing Sleet could hear me. "I'm sorry about that little misunderstanding. I thought you'd like a hard lolly. After all, they last longer. That's why they were one of my favorites growing up."

"Go away," he shouted. "Leave me be."

"I'd love to, but unfortunately students are coming back to school soon. So we need to take you somewhere else. They can't let you stay here, not with classes. I have come to make a deal. Come with me, and I'll make sure your stomach has all the delicious treats you can handle. Or stay here and I promise eventually someone else a lot bigger and meaner than me will show up."

"Certainly couldn't get much older or fatter," he shouted from the pantry.

"Hey," I shouted back. "Now that's just rude."

I worked while I spoke, mixing the sugar, flour, and eggs into the bowl. When it reached the right consistency, I sprinkled the choc chips and started spooning the dough onto the tray. It took me a minute or two to fill the tray and press them with a fork but soon they were all in the oven.

"We might have gotten off on the wrong foot, Sleet, but we can fix that. I'll be here waiting whenever you want to talk."

I reached into my bag and pulled out the Otherworld journal. After all, I had time to kill and so I lifted myself onto the bench and sat there reading while the cookies baked. It didn't take long for the aroma of baking cookies to waft through the kitchen. I'd only made it a handful of chapters when the timer went off on the oven.

Leaping down off the bench, I stopped the buzzer.

"Did you hear that? I think they're done," I called, loud enough to be heard anywhere in the building.

The pixie didn't reply but when I opened the oven a flood of delicious cookie aroma floated through the kitchen. There wasn't a living creature within a hundred meters that wouldn't be able to smell that. I lifted the tray of cookies out of the oven. It wasn't a complex recipe; in fact it was one of the few things I could cook, but as I looked down at them, I couldn't help but feel some pride in my work. They were mouthwatering.

"Damn I'm good." I broke one of the cookies in half and blew on it to cool it. "Some people like them cold with a glass of milk. But me, I like it warm and crumbly so I can taste the melted chocolate on my tongue."

I popped the cookie into my mouth and bit into it. Fresh warm cookie goodness flowed through me.

"That hit the spot. Maybe I'll have another."

I paused, my hand hovering over the tray. "Unless of course you'd like to try one."

The pantry cracked open once more. His little aqua eye regarded me warily. He said nothing, but sniffed as the pungent aroma drew him out of the pantry more effectively than tear gas. I took a plate out of the cupboard, placed a cookie on it, and made my way toward the pantry.

He darted back inside, slamming the door shut.

"Relax, I'm not going to hurt you, Sleet. I'm just gonna pop this down here and head back to my book. Feel free to give it a try. First one is free. After that, we can talk."

I'd barely picked up my book when the pantry door cracked open. Sleet raced out of the pantry like Sylvester chasing Tweety Bird. He darted to the plate, snatched up the cookie, and retreated to the safety of his fortress.

"Careful. It's hot," I called after him. "I don't want you to burn your tongue on it."

There was no response, but a series of chomping bite sounds echoed from the pantry.

When the chomping ceased, a stale silence settled over the kitchen. Sleet had to have finished by now, but it seemed the little pixie was playing hard to get.

"Okay, if you don't want to talk, I guess I'll just have to take these with me." I opened the zip on my duffel, pulled out a small Tupperware container, and started loading the cookies into it.

I'd barely gotten half of them into the container when the door cracked open, and Sleet stuck his head out. He regarded me with a gaze that was equal parts skepticism and greed. The way Scrooge McDuck might look at Bitcoin.

"You're taking them with you?" he asked. "All of them?"

"All of them," I answered. "Unless of course we make a deal. If we do, they could all be yours."

I held up the container. It was transparent and jam-packed with cookies. "Think of all that chocolaty goodness."

The pixie's little tongue wagged like Bran's on a hot day.

"What kind of deal, exactly?"

I crouched down so that I was closer to his eye level. "The school needs you out of here to start classes. They have sent me to take care of it. They're going to give me money, provided I can take you with me. I don't want to hurt you. I just want to take you somewhere else. Hell, we can go anywhere you want, other than here."

"And you'll give me the cookies?" he asked, pointing at the container.

"All of them. As long as you come with me." I held out the container and he inched closer. "There's only one condition."

"And what is that?" he asked.

"You must pretend that I've captured you. They need to believe that you are my prisoner."

He took a step back, "But I don't want to be a prisoner."

"And you won't be. We'd just be pretending," I said, lowering the cookies toward him. "It's like a game. You come with me. I give you the cookies, and I take you somewhere safe. Wherever you want to go. If it goes well, I might even be able to make more cookies."

"More cookies?" Sleet asked, as if they were precious treasure.

"Definitely, but I need money to buy the ingredients. That's why we have to pretend."

"I like cookies." Sleet grinned. "Cookies are delicious."

"We have a deal?"

He nodded and reached up his hand. I took it and shook it with one finger. A tingle of icy power shot up my arm before dissipating.

"Deal," Sleet said.

I gave him the cookies, and then pulled a small bird cage out of the duffel bag. It belonged to Conor's pet parakeet, or at least it did until he let it out for some fresh air. He'd been too young to understand it wouldn't come back. The cage had been gathering dust in the garage ever since.

I opened the door.

"Pop in here. It'll just be a moment, I promise. Once we get out to the car, I'll let you go or give you a lift somewhere else if you want it."

"Promise?" Sleet asked, his voice softening.

"Of course," I replied. "I'm a woman of my word. Even if I'm an old fat one."

The pixie bit his lip as he looked at the floor. "I'm sorry Sleet was rude."

"Let's put that behind us, huh?"

Sleet said nothing, but leapt into the cage. I slid the cookies in behind him and closed the door. Carrying the cage in one hand, I slipped the duffel over my shoulder and made my way out of the kitchens.

I could barely contain my excitement. I'd done it. My very first contract, and I'd done it.

Sleet was in my care and the school was about to become a vandal-free zone.

I smiled all the way to the office.

"Is that him?" Janine asked, angling for a better look at the pixie in the cage.

"Sure is." I gloated. "Let Principal Dare know, would you?"

"You can tell him yourself. I think he's just about out. His door opened a moment ago."

I couldn't resist the urge to do a victory lap, so with the birdcage in one hand, I made my way around the corner of the office. As I did, a familiar voice filtered through the office. There was a condescension to it that was unmistakable.

Naerine of the Summer Court was visible through the door that was slightly ajar.

The hairs on the back of my neck stood on end, and Sleet tried to muffle a gasp.

"The Summer Court would be more than happy to take care of your pixie problem," Naerine said. "After all, he's of the Winter Court and is trespassing on our land. We'll deal with it, swiftly."

Sleet's eyes went wide as he clasped both hands over his mouth.

"That's kind of you, but a hunter showed up earlier. It should already be well in hand," Principal Dare said.

"Hunter?" Naerine asked. "Alasdair?"

Dare shook his head. I retreated from view before he could spot me. "No, someone else. She's one of the parents here. I suspect she joined the Camp recently."

"Take me to her," Naerine demanded. "I met her and Alasdair yesterday. Something is off about her. I have questions I would have answered."

Rather than waiting to be discovered, I raced for the front door. If she'd been suspicious before, seeing me carrying a Winter Court pixie rather than killing it was only going to make her more skeptical.

I stopped dead, shrinking back around the corner lest I be seen. What was I going to do?

I didn't trust the Summer Court as far as I could throw them. The thought of being interrogated by Naerine Oakside caused my heart to pound.

Chapter 12

My heart rate went through the roof. Why was Naerine more interested in me than Sleet?

As the churning sensation settled in my gut, I knew I didn't want to find out. Clutching my duffel with one hand and the cage in the other, I raced for the front door.

"Wait, aren't you going to show Principal Dare?" Janine called from behind the desk.

"Unfortunately, I've got another appointment," I called back.

Showing them my hard-won prize might salve my wounded pride and prove him wrong about me, but I had the distinct impression that it would go poorly for both Sleet and me. Shoving open the front door, I raced along the concrete path to the car park. I glanced back over my shoulder to check if Naerine was on my tail. With any luck, Naerine and Dare would be heading in the other direction, expecting me to be in the kitchens.

Reaching my car, I fumbled in my pocket for my keys and finally managed to mash the button for the central locking. Huffing and puffing, I ripped open the back door, tossed my duffel on the rear, and stuck the birdcage up front in the passenger seat.

"I thought you said you were going to let me go?" the pixie asked.

"And I am, as soon as we're safely away from here. In the meantime, I have a few questions of my own. Like why are the Summer Sidhe looking for you?"

Sleet folded his arms. "I am a creature of Winter. We serve different masters."

I knew that much just from reading the journal. The Sidhe courts were opposite in nature and vying for power, but they didn't live in a state of outright war. So why did Naerine's visit feel so intentional? There was something going on here, a larger picture that I still couldn't see.

"I knew that much," I replied, jamming my key into the ignition and firing up my car. "What I want to know is why she's looking for you in particular. How did she know to find you here?"

I stomped on the accelerator and the car launched forward, spitting gravel behind it.

"Summer and Winter often seek to hinder the other. But such things are above my station," Sleet said. "Summer hates it when Winter enters their domain. But with Summer coming, we don't have any choice."

Summer coming? Was Sleet talking about the seasons? It was spring, now. Summer would be here in a few weeks.

Weaving through the suburban streets, I glanced at the little pixie. It was difficult to tell whether he was intentionally being vague or the detail and subtlety of the Sidhe courts was simply lost on him.

I decided to try another tack, something he'd know more about. He was, after all, the very first creature I'd met from the Otherworld who hadn't tried to kill me.

He reached into the Tupperware container, pulled out a cookie and, holding it in both his little hands, sunk his teeth into it. His enthusiastic groan of approval reminded me of Conor.

"These are very good." Crumbs flew everywhere as he devoured the cookie.

"You've never had cookies before?" I asked, wondering what sort of treats existed in the Otherworld.

Sleet shook his head. "I haven't been here long, only a few days."

"And what exactly are you doing here in Beenleigh? Why here?"

"My master is looking for something," he whispered.

"And you're trying to help him find it?"

The pixie shrugged. "Not particularly."

I looked to Sleet for an explanation.

"The master is very cruel. And I don't like it. I do enough so that he leaves me alone and nothing more. So when he went to the school, I ran away. No more master, many more treats."

"For now, perhaps," I replied, making my way through town, constantly checking my mirror for any sign that I was being followed. "But what do you suppose your master will do when he finds out you have run away?"

"Oh, he's much, much too busy to worry about me." Sleet swallowed as he polished off the cookie. "He is on an errand for the Winter King, and he can't waste time looking for Sleet. Especially if Summer is hunting him. So Sleet escaped. Sleet will be free!"

I had to admire his plan. It seemed he'd picked his moment carefully.

"Does your master have a name?" I asked. "And do you know what he's looking for? His minions are making a mess of the town."

"He's looking for something the Winter King wants very badly. When the Winter King wants something, he sends his Hunter."

"And who is he?"

The pixie fished about in the container for another cookie. For such a small creature, he had a voracious appetite.

"The Red Cap," Sleet said, his fingers closing around a loose choc chip before he popped it in his mouth.

The car screeched to a halt as I stomped on the brakes and pulled over. The vehicle behind me braked, before swerving around me. Popping on my hazard lights, I turned to Sleet.

"The Red Cap? You work for the Red Cap, and you only thought to mention that now?"

The pixie shrugged, somehow not grasping the seriousness of his own words.

"You only asked about it now." He scratched at his temple with one sharp nail. "If you want to know things, you need to ask."

I groaned. The most dangerous creature on the Camp's wanted list and I'd just kidnapped his minion. What was more, I was running from the Summer Court, the people most likely to be able to protect me from him. I had half a mind to turn around and head right back to the school. I had no desire to draw the Red Cap's ire. Perhaps I should hand over Sleet and hope for the best.

But Naerine had been asking about me, and until I knew what that was about, I didn't want to risk it.

Which left me with Sleet, and the Red Cap.

And the Red Cap had already killed Levi Toa, the teacher who had been moonlighting as a bounty hunter. Levi was almost half my age, and twice my size. The Red Cap wouldn't think twice about coming for me.

My hands shook as I gripped the wheel.

What should I do? What *could* I do?

I was caught between the rival courts of the Sidhe, and it was barely past breakfast. My attempt to solo a bounty was going splendidly. No doubt Alasdair was going to have a lot to say about it.

I couldn't sit here forever, and I couldn't go back to the school. Besides, who knew what the Summer Court would do with Sleet?

As annoying as he could be, he was also kind of cute. The little bugger was growing on me. Not knowing how they would treat him, I couldn't do that to him.

Besides, he might know more about his master's business. The sort of information that might give the Camp a leg up on finding him.

But I also didn't want the Red Cap looking for him.

"You said your master is good at finding things. Can't he find you when he finishes his errand for the Winter King?"

Sleet shook his head. "I know all his tricks. He couldn't find me even if he wanted to."

"Well, he knows you were at the school. He could start there?"

"He was at the school when I lost him," Sleet said. "We little folk know how to hide very well. You only found me because I wasn't trying to hide."

"So he's too busy to come looking for you and even if he did, he couldn't find you?"

"That's right." Sleet chortled. "Now it's just me and the cookies."

I put on the indicator and pulled back into traffic, my heartbeat slowing just a little.

"Provided your boss doesn't show up and kill us both," I muttered.

"Where are we going?" Sleet asked.

I cut through town, making a beeline for the Camp. "I need to show you to my boss so that I can collect the bounty."

"Bounty?" the pixie asked as he held up a cookie, examining it more closely. Then he picked out a chocolate chip and popped it in his little mouth. "What's a bounty?"

"Kinda like a job," I replied. "You were tearing up the school and the principal needed you out. They offered money to fix things. Now that I have you with me, I can go collect the money."

"And the money?" the pixie asked. "It buys us more cookies?"

"Sure does," I replied. "It also pays the rent, fuels the car, and keeps the lights on."

"You need money for that?" He squinted up at me, and I had my doubts about whether he understood the concept. Which led me to wonder just how things worked in Faerie. They had to have some sort of currency, surely.

"This money," he said, drumming his fingers against the cookie, "how do we get more of it?"

I laughed, fairly confident that he was trying to ensure his cookie supply line went uninterrupted. "It starts with you playing ball when we meet the Old One."

"Playing ball?"

"Not actual ball." I shook my head. "I need you to pretend I caught you. If he thinks I simply bribed you with the cookies, I might not get this job, and who knows if I'll get the money."

"It's a cunning plan," Sleet said. "You don't lie about it. You just put me in the cage and let their minds tell the lie. You are more like the Sidhe than you realize."

I wasn't sure whether that was a compliment or an insult, but his assessment that my plan was clever did do some good in bolstering my flagging self-esteem. I pulled into the car park behind the Camp, killed the engine, and took Sleet and his cage with me.

I pushed on the door to the building, but it didn't budge.

Locked.

I knocked on it half a dozen times, while glancing back over my shoulder to make sure we weren't being followed. Despite the pixie's reassurances, I was now worried about having both the Summer and Winter Court after me. I didn't want to consider what might happen if I was caught between the two.

"I'm coming, I'm coming," the gurgling voice of the Old One called.

The door opened just a crack, its chain holding it in place. One gloved hand held the door knob, the other stood just out of sight behind the door. I suspected his knife might well be in it. The Old One clearly had either a little paranoia, or an abundance of caution. Perhaps the two stemmed from the same source, an abundance of time spent in the field as a hunter.

"Nora." There was pleasant surprise in his voice. "When you didn't come in this morning, I thought you'd changed your mind."

"On the contrary," I replied, holding up the cage with Sleet in it. "I've just been taking care of my first bounty."

The Old One leaned forward, studying the cage. At that moment, I would have given just about anything to know what he was thinking, but with that veil obscuring his face, I was kept in the dark.

Sleet sniffed at the air and then scurried to the back of the cage, placing as much distance between himself and the Old One as he could.

"Interesting," the Old One mused. "Alasdair will be most displeased."

He let out a gurgling laugh before unchaining the door. As it swung open, I caught the flash of silver as he tucked the knife back into his belt. Well, at least I was right on that count. Perhaps I did have the instincts for this job after all.

I followed him into the Camp, wondering what exactly Alasdair had to be unhappy about. I took a bounty. No one else seemed interested in this particular job as even me, an amateur, had managed to take care of it in a single morning.

"Captain Cranky Pants, upset… who'd have thought? Pray tell, what have I done to offend his sensibilities now?"

"I dare say he'll just be disappointed that you didn't heed his warning, and that you seem intent on pursuing your current course."

"What's wrong with that? Obviously I'm managing just fine." I shook the cage just a little and Sleet let out a shriek of protest. "Just because I'm a little older doesn't mean I can't do this. What have I got to do to prove myself around here?"

"It's not that," the Old One replied, sitting down at the table. A cup of tea rested on a saucer before him. It had a strange herbal smell I didn't recognize and little pieces of green floated in it. It reminded me of the soups with the seaweed floating in them they served in Japanese restaurants.

"Then what is it?" I asked, taking a seat and setting the cage on the table.

"It's not my story to share," the Old One replied. "If you want to know what Alasdair's problem is, you'll have to ask him."

"I did, yesterday, and he didn't say a damn thing," I replied as I caught a glimpse of my reflection in the polished aluminum table. My hair looked like a possum had made a nest in it. Probably a result of my duel with Sleet in the kitchens.

"Men seldom talk about their feelings." The Old One picked up his teacup. "I would have thought you knew that at your age."

My *age*? Apart from his title, I wouldn't have thought us that far apart in age, and yet, I couldn't shake the feeling that we were. It served to remind me just how little I knew about the Old One. Perhaps I could get him talking over a cuppa.

I pointed to the small jug in the middle of the table. "Mind if I have a tea?"

"I doubt it will be to your taste, but by all means."

I made my way to the kitchenette and grabbed a cup, a saucer, and a napkin before returning to the table and pouring myself a cup of the steaming brew. Holding it to my nose, I took a deep breath. It was heady, earthy, and aromatic, but still I couldn't place it.

Tentatively, I took a sip.

It was like sucking on moss covered in pond scum. Perhaps one that had sat fermenting in a shallow pool of fetid water for a decade.

I spat the mouthful of tea back into the cup.

"Oh my." I groaned, setting it back on the table. "That is foul. How can you even drink that?"

Sticking out my tongue, I tried to scrape any residue of the brew from it with the napkin.

"I tried to warn you," the Old One replied. "One of these days, you're going to need to start listening to those."

"Warnings?" I asked.

"Yes. You cannot afford to try and learn every lesson the hard way, Nora. One of them is going to kill you."

I chafed at the chastisement. I'd spent years being told what to do by my husband. Now the pendulum had swung back hard in the other direction. I didn't want to be told; I just wanted to work it out myself.

Not in the mood to swallow my pride just yet, I changed the topic. Pointing at the cage, I asked, "Does this mean I am a hunter now? I got my first bounty."

The Old One glanced from Sleet to the bounty board, and then the gold coins beneath it.

"Not quite," he replied.

I knew it. Shifting the goalposts. No sooner had I cleared the bar then they moved it to make things harder.

Grimacing as I tried to hide my disappointment, I sat up a little straighter. "How did I know that you would say that? You said that when I take a bounty, I would pass the third test."

"No," the Old One replied. "I said when you take your first head. You've merely run an errand, child, one for which you will be paid. But we are hunters here, not errand runners. Hence why that contract has sat untouched for days. Hunters hunt. We kill our prey, the Sidhe invaders who trespass in this world. We are the blade that prevents trouble from that realm spilling over here into the wilds. We are the last line of defense. If you wish to be a hunter, you must be able to take a life."

The Old One produced his knife and set it on the table before me. It was black and seemed to be fashioned from a single piece of dark metal. Iron perhaps, or something else.

Sleet let out a shrill squeak and shook the door of the cage. "You promised!"

I looked at the knife but didn't take it.

"That's what I thought," the Old One replied. "Now you have two problems."

"How do you figure that?" I asked, leaning back in my chair. I wasn't murdering a hapless pixie who had just gotten out of an abusive relationship. It struck too close to home.

The Old One lowered his head until he was eye level with Sleet beating on the door of his cage.

"You've captured one of the Winter Court's scouts, and now it knows you don't have the stomach to kill it."

"He wants no part of the Court," I replied. "He wants to be free."

The Old One let out a gurgling laugh.

"You think the Court cares what it wants? Or what *you* want?" The Old One shook his head. "You have taken something that doesn't belong to you. You have left neutral ground, Nora Byrne, and Winter will come for you."

Chapter 13

The Old One's warning sent a shiver down my spine. While I understood his words, I didn't want to believe them.

What if I just let the pixie go? All I would have done was moved the pixie from one place to another. What was it to them? There was still so much about the Courts of the Sidhe that I didn't understand.

"Why me?" I stammered. "I don't understand. Why would they care? All I did was move him."

"And what now?" the Old One asked. "If you keep him, you'll be harboring a creature of Winter. You will have taken something that belongs to the Winter King for yourself. If you turn him loose, mindless creature that he is, Summer will invariably kill him. You will be blamed for his loss. Sidhe masters have obligations to their underlings to see to their protection. His will demand an answer. Will you be ready to give it?"

"His master is the Red Cap." I groaned, a sickening sensation settling in my stomach.

"I suspected as much," the Old One replied. "Their presence here together can't be a coincidence. Take the knife and do what must be done. Earn your coin. If you're a hunter, they might think twice."

I looked at the knife resting in the middle of the table. The Old One was trying to protect me, after his fashion. I could see that now. But I couldn't do what he wanted.

There had to be another way. I looked at Sleet cowering at the back of his cage.

"His Master is the Red Cap," the Old One said, "and you and I both know he won't think twice about coming for a hunter."

I bit my lip as I considered what might come of the path I was walking.

"I gave my word that I would not harm him. I can't break it."

The Old One let out an awkward click as he studied me through his veil. "I don't suppose you can."

"Where does that leave us?" I asked, feeling far less comfortable about my morning's work than I had half an hour ago.

"We wait, we watch, and we hunt," the Old One answered. "And in the meantime, you pay your rent. Where would you like the money sent?"

"The bounty?" I asked. It wasn't much but every bit helped right now.

"Yes. Give me your account details and I'll have the funds released immediately." The Old One pulled a small notepad from the folds of his black robes and slid it across the table.

Taking it and pulling a pen from my pocket, I jotted down my bank details.

"That's something." I managed a smile but my heart wasn't in it. At least I could clear a little of the rent I owed. Hopefully get the landlord off my back.

"It'll be in your account in an hour. In the meantime, I suggest you go home and think carefully about your little friend there."

"Why? As far as I can tell, he is only dangerous to things that contain sugar."

"Looks can be deceiving," the Old One replied. "Learn that quickly. Perhaps more than any other lesson. It might just save your life."

The Old One folded his arms across his chest. "You really don't know, do you?"

"Know what?" I asked, growing weary of the Camp and his secrets.

The Old One shook his head. "It's not my place to say. Perhaps it's better this way."

He rose from the table, taking his tea with him.

"What's better? Tell me, please," I said. "I need answers, not more questions."

He waved a gloved hand and headed for the back office, clearly finished with our conversation.

"What am I meant to do? Take the day off? I was hoping to get some training," I called after him.

"One lesson a day is more than enough," he called back. "Besides, Alasdair is busy, and I have nothing else I would give you unsupervised. So go home and enjoy your win. And give consideration to whether or not this is truly what you want. If you want to be a hunter, you have a decision to make. Wishing will only get you so far, Nora Byrne."

The Old One shut the door behind him. I sat there at the table, looking from the cup of foul-tasting tea to Sleet still cowering in his cage.

"You said you were going to release me." He stared at me, his little head cocked to one side, his lip quivering. "I trusted you."

I held up a hand for quiet as I picked up the cage and made my way out to the car. Once we'd cleared the Camp I turned to Sleet.

"I trusted you, too. It turns out we may have to keep trusting each other, because I'm certainly not going to kill you in spite of the fact that everyone keeps telling me I should. They certainly think your old master's going to kill us."

"He is not nice," Sleet replied in perhaps the greatest understatement of the day. He seemed so calm about the Red Cap. Perhaps living with the threat of his old master had simply become a fact of life for the little creature.

"Well, I'm certainly not him," I said, reaching down and opening the cage. "So, like I promised, you're free to go."

Sleet clutched the only remaining cookie in his hands and looked at me, then looked at the empty container. He didn't seem to be in any real hurry to leave.

"Go on then, you're free." I stood there with the cage resting on the top of my car, but the little pixie just didn't budge.

"What's wrong?" I asked, leaning a little closer. "This is what you wanted, right?"

Sleet sat down, biting into his cookie.

"Sleet wasn't at the school to cause trouble." He looked down at the floor of the cage. "Sleet was there because he didn't have any other place to go."

His lip quivered and my heart just about broke for the little guy. Here I was worrying about paying rent. He didn't even have a home. He'd spent so much of his life enslaved by a cruel master. Now he might be free, but he was homeless too.

I felt a little guilty. I had never really considered why he was there, or even asked. I couldn't just leave him here, helpless, in a world he didn't understand.

"Well, if Sleet is looking for somewhere to stay, there is always room at my place," I said.

He looked up at me, lip trembling, big tears welling in his eyes. "Really?"

"Sure," I replied. "We're already in the firing line. We may as well stick together."

Sleet clearly wanted nothing to do with his old master and while the thought of the Red Cap scared the hell out of me, I couldn't let the fear of it keep me from living. Besides, I was pretty sure Conor and Shay would find Sleet to be a riot. After all, the two of them had always wanted to adopt every stray we came across. That was how we got Bran in the first place.

"Sure, if you want somewhere safe to hide out, you're welcome to stay with us. At least until you find something that you prefer more."

Sleet stared down into the empty container of cookies. With his deceptively large appetite, I imagined he was already concerned about where his next cookie was coming from. Another mouth to feed was going to complicate things, but he couldn't be worse than Conor. The boy ate like a linebacker.

Sleet stepped out of the cage and, with a beat of his wings, shot at me like a rocket. I drew back, ready to swat him out of the air with a slap. He wrapped his little arms around my neck and hugged me.

"Will there be cookies?" he asked, hope hanging in every syllable.

"Yes, but not for breakfast," I answered sternly. "Too much of a good thing can be a bad thing, you know."

"I see," he said in a voice so filled with skepticism, I truly doubted it.

I tossed the empty cage in the back seat and motioned to the passenger seat. "If you want to ride up front, you're more than welcome."

Sleet zipped into the front seat and sat there, rocking slowly.

"You're going to have to buckle up, buddy. I don't know if you've been in many car rides, but if we have an accident, you're going to go flying."

Sleet looked up at me, his face screwed up in confusion. "But I fly all the time."

"It's the stop at the end of the flight that's the problem." I laughed. "You'll hit that window and could get hurt."

Unfortunately, his miniature frame was simply too small to use the belt effectively. I plugged the belt in for him, but it sat above his head. I had to laugh. He was little bigger than a toy, sitting in the massive seat, but there was no mistaking the smile on his lips.

"Hmm, we're going to have to do something about that for next time."

I pulled out of the parking lot, hunger gnawing at me. As we passed the local Bunnings, I decided to do something about it. As we pulled in, the smell of cooking onions and sausages wafted through the open windows.

There was nothing that smelled quite as good as a sausage sizzle. And in Australia, for whatever reason, it seemed every hardware store had one on every Saturday. What better to lure hungry shoppers in than the pungent aroma of a BBQ. It was a marketing ploy that was as devious as it was genius.

Bunnings, the giant hardware chain, had a reputation for its sausage sizzles being both cheap and delicious. I wasn't sure what made their snags better. Perhaps it was magic, but they always hit the spot.

I parked near the door. I had no intention of going inside today. I just wanted a snack.

I looked at Sleet. Explaining his presence would be difficult for those who didn't believe in the Otherworld, and that was most people.

"Just stay here. I'll be back in a minute with something to eat."

That seemed to reassure him as I shut the door and made my way to the gazebo beside the Bunnings' entrance. The aroma of sausages was even stronger here and my stomach churned in anticipation.

"What can I get you?" asked the cashier, a young man in his late teens. He was wearing a shirt with a logo for one of the local rugby clubs. It seemed fund-raising for the next season had begun.

"Three sausages on bread, please, with onions and barbecue sauce."

"Sure thing." The man punched it into an EFTPOS machine. "That will be seven-fifty."

I pulled out my wallet, took out my credit card, and tapped it against the machine. I glanced at the hotplates laden with sausages and onion. The aroma ensured a steady stream of customers filling the line behind me.

It only took a minute before three sausages were placed neatly on bread, smothered in onion, and lined up in a neat little silver holder ready for collection.

"The sauce is there on the table. Have as much as you like."

I doused two of the sausages in BBQ sauce while wondering what the Sidhe might think of it.

"If he doesn't like it, I guess it's three for me." I laughed as I doused it, too. I lifted the three sausages, sandwiched them in one hand, and pulled my keys out my pocket as I headed for the car.

Opening the door. I slid into the seat and turned to Sleet who was already eying the sausages.

"What is it?" he asked, leaning toward me.

"It's a sausage sizzle, Sleet. An Australian special. You're just not living until you've had a Bunnings snag."

I handed him one of the sausages and without hesitation, he bit an inch long section off the end of the steaming hot sausage.

The pixie announced his pleasure with a groan. "Almost as good as cookies."

"High praise, indeed," I replied, biting into my own.

We sat there in silence, wolfing down our sausages. I finished my first one. To my surprise, his sausage and bread were entirely gone, and he was licking his fingers.

The sight was giving me some reservations as to what the little guy might do to my grocery budget.

Sleet eyed the second one. I'd gotten it for myself, but I couldn't stand to see him go hungry.

"Want this one?" I raised an eyebrow as I held it out.

His grin only broadened. "Yes, please."

I tore the sausage and bread in half and handed it over.

"I'm sure the kids are going to love you."

"Kids?"

"Yep, I have two kids waiting for us at home. I'm sure you'll love them."

"More friends," he said happily.

I shook my head. "Not just friends, family, Sleet. If you are living with us, then you're family. We'll take care of you, but you have to watch out for us too. That's what family do. They take care of each other, do you understand?"

Sleet nodded.

"Have you ever had a family?"

"Not for a long time," he said, his lip quivering.

"Well, you are welcome to be a part of mine. But, know this, my family is the most important thing in the world to me. There is nothing I won't do to protect them. If you or anyone else brings harm to them, I won't hesitate to do exactly what the Old One suggested. Do you understand?"

Sleet nodded and swallowed slowly.

"Good, and if you are a part of that family, that goes for you too. I'll do what I can to keep you safe."

I slid the key into the ignition. It was good that we understood each other, because if there was any guile behind that little smile, I wanted him to know the measure of my resolve.

Pulling into my driveway, I parked the car.

"We're home. Let me do the talking, okay?"

Sleet nodded tentatively and clutched his empty Tupperware container. I leaned over and undid his seatbelt. He didn't move. Figuring he might have some trepidation, I let him be. I wound down the window so he could come in whenever he was ready.

I made my way to the house. As I pushed open the door, Sleet zipped out the open window, crossed the lawn in a flash, and landed on my shoulder like a blue and purple parrot. Giving him a reassuring smile, we stepped inside.

Laughter trickled out of the living room, and we followed it to the source. My mother sat on the couch watching cartoons with Conor. Shay was curled up in the recliner reading her book.

They hadn't heard me over the sound of the TV, so I figured I'd make the most of it.

"What are you watching?" I asked as I crouched down behind Conor.

"Mum!" He turned, and his gaze drifted to the little blue form perched on my shoulder. His big blue eyes almost burst out of his head.

"Conor, meet Sleet."

"A pixie," Conor shrieked.

How had he known that?

I turned to face my mother, who was yet to say a word. I'd expected her to have strong feelings about the presence of a genuine creature from the Otherworld.

Shay looked up from her book, a Nancy Drew mystery, and almost fell off the recliner.

"He's so cute," she squealed. "Can we keep him?"

"Sleet is going to be staying with us for a while, so why don't you two show him around the house?"

Both of them jumped to their feet, and I motioned to Sleet. "It's okay. They'll take good care of you."

"Come on upstairs, I'll show you my room," Conor said as he held out his hand.

Sleet flitted over to Conor and the three of them took off up the stairs.

When they'd disappeared, I turned to Mom. "We need to talk."

"Nora." My mother's voice was quiet, almost timid, not her usual unflappable self. "What have you done?"

That was the question of the day. What exactly had I done?

I'd taken a bounty, met a pixie, and brought him home to join my family. I'd also likely antagonized his master, the Red Cap.

Things were happening so quickly, I was struggling to keep up with them myself. I hadn't said a word to her about what I'd been doing, other than mentioning the ice troll Alasdair and I had tackled at the library.

Frankly, I was a little worried about how she was going to take the news. Her hands were shaking, and I wasn't sure what to make of her subdued state. She'd always been mindful of the Otherworld, but one look at Sleet had reduced her to silence. What was she so afraid of?

"Mum, this is going to be a lot to take in. But when the library closed, I started looking for work. I kind of got mixed up with the bounty hunter who saved me at the library."

"A hunter? Nora, you didn't," my mother whispered. "I've warned you about the Otherworld,"

"Yes, you have," I said. I didn't need another lecture right now. "But that hasn't stopped it from trying to kill me. I don't know how to explain it, Mum, but it was like that troll was drawn to me. And I can't just ignore its existence now that I know it's there. It's like there's a part of me that needs to know more about it. Working with Alasdair gives me a chance to learn."

"Alasdair, the man on the bike?"

"Yeah." I smoothed my clammy palms against my jeans. "He's the one who saved my life in the library."

"So he's to blame for all this?"

I shook my head. "No, Mum, if he had his way, I wouldn't be anywhere near it."

"Then why are you?"

The abruptness of her question caught me off guard.

I stared down at my lap, unable to meet her steely gaze. It was hard to explain why I was doing something that brought with it such great risks. The money was one thing. It was certainly what I'd been telling myself and anyone else who would listen, but it ran deeper than that.

"I don't know how to describe it, Mum. I just feel like I need to do this."

My mom sighed. "All my life I have been trying to protect you from this. I have moved continents, uprooted my life, and worn out my lungs warning you of the perils of those creatures and still you have found your way to them."

I could hear the disappointment in her voice and that hurt most of all.

"I know they're not to be trusted."

"It's not just that, Nora. We didn't move to Australia for the warmer climate, dear. We moved here to get as far away from the Winter Court as I could manage, and still be on the same planet."

"I get it."

"Do you?" she countered. "Because after decades of being off their radar, you appear to have stolen one of their little folk and brought him into your home. You have no idea what you've done."

Here she was, doing it again. She was always willing to tell me what I should and shouldn't do but not why. Forty years of being kept in the dark boiled up within me.

"You're right, Mum. I have no idea." I raised my voice. "Because you won't tell me. Every time I try to understand what's going on, you keep me in the dark."

She looked away, and I took a breath to try and calm myself.

"You don't tell me why. You just tell me what. And I need more. They're here, the Winter and Summer Courts, and being in the dark is what is going to get me killed. Tell me why you are so afraid of them? What did they do to you?"

My mother's steely gray eyes glistened as her Irish stubbornness wavered.

"Everything, dear," she said. "They did everything to me, and it was all I could do to escape with my life."

"What do you mean escape?"

My mother hunched over and patted the cushion beside her. "You're going to want to sit for this."

Reluctantly, I flopped down beside her. I didn't speak. I wasn't letting her off that easily. I wanted answers.

"The reason you feel so drawn to them, Nora, is because you're one of them."

My ears must have been playing tricks on me. My mouth moved, as I searched for words and found none.

"You, my daughter, my precious Nora, are a child of the Winter Court. Why do you think I've tried so hard to hide you from them?"

I went to speak, but my mother held up a hand. "Let me finish."

She fussed at the seam of her pants. "When I was a little girl, I was always fascinated by the stories of the Otherworld, but it wasn't until I was in college that I actually stumbled across it. I was hiking in the hills when I found a set of stones. I'd heard the stories about those who had passed through such and entered the Otherworld, but I figured them for a myth. As I wandered between them, the Veil parted and I found myself in a land of ice and snow."

"Faerie," I whispered.

"Yes," my mother replied. "I'd been drawn in by their magic and was taken by the Winter Court. You cannot truly understand their nature without living among them, Nora. I did. And they are nothing like us. Lithe but powerful, graceful yet fearsome. Noble but terrible and their mood shifts like the sea. They are captivating to us mortals. One of the Sidhe noticed me."

She sighed. "He showed me wonders I had never imagined, and foolish girl that I was, I became his consort. Looking back, I don't know that I had much choice in the matter. I lived there for years until one day the impossible happened. I learned that I was pregnant, with you.

"Knowing the nature of that place and the part you would play in it, I conspired with my lover's servants to flee whilst he was seeing to the duties of the Court. The pixies took me and spirited me back through the stones. I ran, Nora. I ran for all I was worth. For whatever else I'd found in Faerie, I would happily give it all away to keep you safe."

"I don't understand." My hands shook, and I pressed them into my lap. "You're telling me my father is one of the Sidhe?"

"Yes," she whispered.

My mind reeled. Had that been what Alasdair and the Old One had been talking about? Did they know what I was? I recalled meeting the Summer Sidhe in the grove. Naerine had said something about Winter. Had she sensed it? My nature? Was that even possible? Alasdair had said something about the ice troll. Had he just been covering for me?

If so, everything was starting to make more sense.

"And that's where I get my powers," I said, unable to fathom the depths of the secrets my mother had been keeping.

"Yes," she replied.

"Who was he?" I demanded. "You told me he was an egomaniac, a workaholic. Now I learn he was a member of the Winter Court. You couldn't have led with that?"

My mother bit her lip. "All of it was true, my dear, just not the whole truth. Your father is many things. I spent years trying to understand him and I barely scratched the surface, but this I know. Your presence would have presented him with a great many challenges and been dangerous for you. Scions are not common."

"Scions?"

"Half-Sidhe. Children born of those who take human companions. I wasn't sure how he'd react, and I didn't want to risk it, Nora. The Sidhe don't abide weakness. They extinguish it. Given the choice between you and him, I chose you."

I couldn't even imagine what that had been like for her, leaving her lover to raise me on her own.

"Who was he?" I asked. "I want a name."

"Nora," my mother warned.

"Tell me who my father was." My voice grew louder with every word. "I want to know."

My mother shook her head. "You can't un-know this, please."

"Tell me." My voice cracked. "Please."

"Your father is Oberon, King of the Winter Court."

An icy chill started in my ears at the very mention of his name and shot through me like a bolt of ice-cold lightning.

The King of the Winter Court. I'd read of him, of course. I'd read all about him in the Otherworld journal. Powerful and terrible, the Sidhe monarch reigned with an iron grip over the icy fields of Winter. His will shaped the very fabric of Faerie itself.

I didn't know what to say.

"Now you can see why I didn't say anything," my mother whispered. "You can't unlearn this, Nora. It will change you, define you, shape you, like it does him. All your life, I've tried to protect you from the terrible burden of your father. I've given everything, and now I fear I've not done enough.

I always feared it would find you, but you've found it and invited it into your home. I suppose it was only a matter of time before it found Conor."

"What are you talking about?" I asked.

"Those things he sketches, they aren't from any game. I have seen them all before, in Winter. Whatever is happening to Conor, his blood—*your* blood—ties him to that place. Sooner or later, they're going to find us. I fear that little pixie is only the beginning."

"I can't throw him out," I said. "I promised I would give him a place to stay, and I won't break that promise."

"I never asked you to," my mother replied. "It wouldn't be right. We have a debt that must be repaid."

"What are you talking about?"

"You said his name was Sleet? I thought I recognized him, though he was just a child when I knew him. Small enough to hide behind one finger." She smiled at the memory. "He looks just like his father."

"You knew his father?" I asked.

"His whole family, though I doubt he recognizes me. Time has been less kind to me. His father, Storm, was the one who helped me escape. Whatever else Sleet might be, I know he comes from a family I owe my life to. That debt must be paid. The real question is why is he here and not there with his family?"

"They're all dead," I replied. "Sleet wouldn't speak of it, but I could tell."

My mother shook her head. "Your father must have discovered the role they played in my escape."

"You can't know that," I replied.

"You don't know him like I do. He'd have had little choice in the matter."

"He's the King of Winter."

"Only as long as he plays the part. The moment he shows weakness, another will try and take his mantle. It is their way."

"Well, it seems Sleet was given to the Red Cap," I replied. "He escaped when they came through the Veil looking for something."

"The Red Cap is here?" My mother bolted upright.

"You know him?" I asked and then felt foolish. Of course, she did. Here I was learning from a journal, when my mother had spent a lifetime living there.

"Everybody knows him," my mother whispered. "He's your father's right hand, his chosen hunter. It can't be a coincidence. Nora, he is not looking for something. He's looking for us. Me, you, your children. He wants you and he'll stop at nothing to bear out his master's will."

My heart hammered in my chest. For days I had been ignoring the Red Cap, hoping he would simply go away, or be driven off by the Summer Court.

Now I realized that was never going to happen.

Sooner or later, he was going to come for me, and when he did, he was going to have the might of the Winter Court behind him.

How the hell was I meant to stop him?

Chapter 14

Sleep proved elusive, and I wasn't particularly surprised. After everything my mother had dropped on me, it was a miracle I managed any at all. On the plus side, being up early had given me a chance to take care of the chores I'd been neglecting around the house the past few days.

I was just finishing a few of the dishes that had piled up when the guttural rumble of a motorbike rolled up outside.

"Mum, your friend is here," Shay called from the living room.

Conor got up from the kitchen bench and made his way to the loungeroom to take a look.

I threw the dish towel over the rack to dry and grabbed my bag.

"Cool motorbike," Conor muttered.

There was only one person I knew that rode a motorbike. Alasdair.

The Old One had said he would get me more training. I wasn't expecting a house call, though. I figured they'd be waiting for me at the Camp.

No one had given me any directions about what time I was expected. I looked at the wall-mounted clock. It was a shade after eight. It felt early. Then again, I didn't really know what hours a bounty hunter was meant to keep. Perhaps something had happened.

Sleet was sitting on the end of the counter eating a bowl of cereal coated in a diabetes-inducing layer of brown sugar. I had no idea if pixies had to worry about that sort of thing but resolved to educate myself. If he was living here, someone needed to look after him.

"Keep an eye on them, Sleet," I said as I headed for the door.

"Both eyes," the pixie replied. "I'll be watching."

He seemed to be taking to his new role as the household's scout with vigor. But the household's real protector was waiting for me in the lounge room.

"He is right, you know. It is a nice motorbike," my mother teased. "The kind of bike ridden by men my mother warned me about."

"Clearly you didn't listen, either," I replied, kissing both children on the forehead as I made my way out the door.

Alasdair sat on the side of the road, his bike idling. Mrs. Grobinsky, ever watchful, was standing in her front yard watering her begonias and judging me silently. I prayed to whatever gods might be listening that she'd forget seeing Alasdair before she had a chance to share it with the entire street.

"Take your sweet time," Alasdair replied as I crossed the lawn.

"If I'd known you were coming, I would have been ready sooner."

"If you're intent on being a hunter, you should always be ready."

The day's lesson. Rather than bicker with him, I was determined to get all the training I could. It seemed my life, and the lives of those I loved, depended on it.

"So where are we off to at this hour?"

"Emergency call," he said. "The boss insists I take you along, and for once, I'm inclined to agree."

He held out the helmet and I slid it over my head, pressing my hair as flat as I could so that it would fit.

"Where are we headed?"

"Back to the scene of your great triumph," Alasdair replied, sarcasm in his voice.

The school. I hadn't really been anywhere else lately. Wrapping my arms around him as I straddled the bike, I reminded myself to stay focused and not dwell on just how good it felt to have my arms wrapped around that strong, well-muscled torso.

The task was made much easier by remembering the irritating things that came out of his mouth nine times out of ten.

He guided the bike through downtown Beenleigh and pulled into the school car park. There were only three vehicles there, but the one that got my attention was the police car, pulled in behind Principal Dare's. Alasdair pulled up to the squad car and got off his bike. As he did, two seasoned officers climbed out to meet him.

"What are we doing here?" I whispered.

My reluctant mentor ignored the question, directing his attention to the police.

"Thanks for the call, gents," Alasdair said. "Is anyone else inside?"

"Just his assistant. She was the one who found him."

"All right, we'll take a look." Alasdair motioned for me to follow him.

The lead officer raised a hand to stop him. "This is too much, Alasdair. We can't keep covering this up. Now we have witnesses."

"Relax, Collins, we're here, aren't we?" Alasdair replied.

The vein in the officer's temple bulged, the color rising in his cheeks. "You look at what they did to him and then tell me to relax. These monsters are killing our people. We can't keep sweeping this under a rug."

"Do as you please," Alasdair replied. "I'm doing everything I can, but we both know the panic that will cause. It will only make both our jobs harder."

Collins dropped his hand. "Make it quick. We'll have to call it in soon."

What exactly had happened here? I climbed off the bike as Alasdair reached into the saddlebags and drew out his leather satchel. I fell in beside him as he headed for the admin block.

"What was all that about?" I asked.

"Things are getting worse."

If there was a gold medal for being vague, my new mentor would be a strong contender.

He pushed open the glass door. Janine stood at her desk, weeping uncontrollably. A handful of tissues formed a small pile in front of her.

"Where is he?" Alasdair asked without any pleasantries.

"In there." She pointed toward Dare's office. "I found him like that when I came in. His wife texted me when he didn't come home last night, so I came in early to see if everything was all right. It wasn't."

Janine crumpled into her chair.

"Stay here," Alasdair said. "Don't let anyone else through while we're inside, do you understand?"

Janine nodded, still sobbing.

Alasdair muttered something that I didn't quite catch, but a tingle ran down my spine. From Janine's warning, I had an idea of what was waiting for us in Dare's office. Following Alasdair's lead, I mustered what power I could, and held it ready.

Compared to Alasdair, I was a featherweight, but every bit counted, just like it had with the troll.

We pushed open the door to Principal Dare's office. My stomach lurched. I wasn't ready for this at all.

I retched and gulped as I fought the urge to vomit.

"Get yourself under control," Alasdair growled. "If we're panicking, it will only make it worse for her."

He nodded in Janine's direction.

Principal Dare lay spreadeagled, tied to his desk and impaled on an immense spike of ice that burst from his chest. It was covered in blood and gore and what I was pretty sure were his entrails draped all over the crystalline shard.

"What the hell?" I muttered. "He was alive when I left him. How could this have happened?"

"I told you to leave it alone," Alasdair replied as he bent down to examine the body. "But you didn't listen, did you? Stubborn woman, always doing what you want. Well, this is what happens when you're ignorant. You get people killed."

"You're blaming *me* for this?" I hissed, slamming the door shut so that Janine couldn't hear us. "How is this my fault?"

"You took the bounty," Alasdair said as he looked up from the corpse. "This is what happens when you fumble about in our world. Why do you think I hadn't bothered with it? A pixie vandalizing a school, it's nothing. Give the creature a few days and it will move on of its own accord. But no, you took the bounty, and hours after you cashed it in, the person responsible for placing it dies, at Winter's hand, no doubt. This is the Red Cap's work."

A shiver ran down my spine at the mention of the creature.

"How can you tell?" I ignored his accusation. It wouldn't do me any good to get him more worked up than he already was.

"Experience," he replied as he studied the principal's corpse. "The pixie was a creature of Winter, likely a scout, and it appears the Red Cap took umbrage with a bounty being placed on one of his own. You should have stayed away, Nora. Why couldn't you have just stayed away?"

"I told you, I need this," I said. "The money from that bounty will put food on the table and cover my rent this week. That troll destroyed the library and my livelihood. Don't think this was the first thing I tried. I looked all over town. There were no jobs anywhere. So I took the smallest bounty, hoping you would see my resolve, and train me, rather than try to drive me off."

"This man is dead because you took it."

"He's dead because that monster killed him. Stop trying to put that on me. You told me it was our job to protect these people. The pixie was terrorizing the school. I took care of it."

"And now the principal is dead," Alasdair replied. "If you're so bloody determined to be a hunter, learn this lesson well. Neutral ground, you've left it. There is no getting back. Principal Dare put a contract on a creature of Winter. That made him a player in the game, and the Red Cap answered. Just like he did against our own hunters. You ought to be running for your life, Nora. If he did this to the man who placed the bounty, what do you think he is going to do to the person who carried it out? It's a miracle you made it through the night."

"You think he'll come for me?" My heart fluttered erratically.

"You took the bounty. Levi Toa simply started asking after the Red Cap and in that beast's eyes that was enough to warrant a response. He's a noble of the Winter Court. We don't have the manpower to take him on. If I were you, I would be terrified."

My hands started shaking. I couldn't help it. I hadn't just taken the bounty; I'd taken Sleet.

"Sooner or later, he's going to come for you, so I hope you learn quickly, Nora, because as of last night, you're probably the top of his most wanted list."

"Is it possible that someone else could have done this?" I asked.

Alasdair folded his arms as he inched around the corpse. He seemed to be doing his utmost to avoid contaminating the scene.

"What makes you say that?

"Because when I left here yesterday, Dare wasn't alone. That Summer Sidhe from the park, Naerine, was here talking with Dare. What if the Summer Court did this? Could they be trying to frame the Red Cap? Perhaps it has nothing to do with me at all? Or maybe the Red Cap was simply retaliating for whatever information the principal gave the Summer Court."

Alasdair considered it. "The Summer Court were here, in this office? Speaking with Dare?"

I nodded, hoping he was wrong about the cause of Dare's death.

"Did you hear what they were talking about?"

"I only caught the tail end. They seemed to be talking about the bounty. Dare mentioned that I was here, and Naerine wanted to speak with me."

Alasdair shook his head. "I don't like this one bit. First the Red Cap's scout is here, sniffing about the school. Now the Summer Court is here too. Whoever did this was trying to send a message. One they hoped we would get."

"What makes you think that?" I asked.

"Because we killed an ice troll the day before yesterday. It was a clear message that while our numbers might be diminished, the hunters are still active. Now we have both Winter and Summer sniffing about, and Summer is asking about you. I fear they might know the truth about you."

"I haven't told a soul," I replied. "I didn't know the truth about myself until last night. Thanks for that, by the way."

"I figured if you didn't know, it wasn't my place to share." Alasdair glanced at the body, then grabbed my hand and pulled me toward the front door. "We need to get out of here, now."

"I don't understand why we're here in the first place," I said, trying not to look at the grotesque form of my kid's principal. "Why did the police call you?"

"They call the Camp when they find crime scenes that might concern us. This definitely qualifies, and the Old One wants to know what went on here. Whatever it is, it seems to be at the heart of what's going on between the Sidhe. But something's not right. This feels like a trap. We need to move."

It just didn't make any sense. Arthur Dare was one of the nicest men I'd ever met. Why would they do something like this to him?

I took one final look at his body. Alasdair might want to run, but if these people were coming for me, I needed to know why. Avoiding the mess that had been made of his midsection, I glanced at his arms. There was a series of cuts down one arm. Not mindless scratches or defensive wounds, but deliberate cuts, each several centimeters long, about a centimeter apart.

They started at his elbow and moved down his arm. I could tell they were intentional, because they had been placed carefully to avoid any major blood vessels, anything that would cause consistent bleeding. In fact, it would be difficult to make so many of them without accidentally slitting one of Arthur's veins and killing him. It showed a grisly attention to detail and a thorough understanding of human anatomy.

At least three of the nails on his left hand had been pulled off.

I held the door, preventing Alasdair from opening it.

"He's been tortured," I muttered.

"What?"

"Look." I pointed to the marks on his arm, and his missing nails. "Whoever it was, they knew what they were doing. They did the most damage possible without actually killing him. They tore out his nails, tortured his arm. They weren't trying to kill him. They were trying to get something out of him. What do you reckon that was?"

After hearing my mother's secret, part of me worried they might be searching for us. The ones who got away. But why now, after all this time?

"Whatever it was, they got it," Alasdair replied.

"What makes you say that?" I asked, studying the body for anything I might have missed.

"Because if they hadn't, they wouldn't have stopped," he said, his thick accent turning gruff and impatient. "Look at the impression on the index finger. They started at the pinky and stopped there. Which means whatever it is they wanted to know, Dare gave it to them."

The image of poor Arthur trapped in his office with the Red Cap, slowly being tortured to death, was a grim one. What had they been looking for?

"We should question his assistant, Janine," I replied. "She was here yesterday. Maybe she overheard something."

"It could be anything for all we know, but if we don't get you out of here, you're dead, Nora. If there was ever a time in your life to listen to me, this is it. Who cares what they wanted from him? You could be next."

"Look, Alasdair, it's not just about me. My children come here; so do others. They are meant to come back to school next week. I can't send them here knowing the forces of Winter could show up at any time."

Alasdair stopped moving. "Wait, your children come here?"

"Yes," I replied. He was finally getting it.

"And you didn't think to mention that until now?" His voice rose.

I pushed my hair back out of my face. "It didn't seem relevant with everything else that was going on."

"Didn't seem relevant." Alasdair was red in the face. "You're going to get us killed; your family too."

I ripped my hand out of Alasdair's. "Stop lecturing me and tell me what the hell is going on. You're meant to be training me, not leaving me in the dark."

"I doubt you'll survive long enough to be trained. Your children come here, to this school. Someone, likely the Red Cap, was torturing the principal, right after you collected a bounty he placed. It's not a far cry to consider that he might be torturing him about your whereabouts. If your kids come here, your address will be on file."

My heart felt like a piece of lead. He was right.

The Red Cap was hunting me, and the school did have my address. They needed it in case anything happened with the children.

Now those children were home with my mother, and the Red Cap could be on his way.

"We need to get out of here, and get you home," Alasdair said, pulling out his phone and heading for the door.

"Who are you calling?"

"The Old One. If they are coming for you, we need all the help we can get."

I didn't need to be pulled along now; I started running for the door.

"Janine, you need to leave now. It's not safe," I said as I raced by her desk.

"I can't leave him," she whispered, looking at the office.

"You'll end up dead next to him if you don't," Alasdair said, right behind me.

She stood there shaking, pale and swaying on her feet.

I felt sorry for her. I knew exactly how she felt. It was how I'd felt two days ago in the library. I hadn't seen my boss dead on the table, but I'd come face to face with my own mortality and only narrowly avoided its embrace.

I halted in front of her desk. "There will be time to cry, but right now, we need to go."

A screech of tires issued from outside. I looked out the window at the car park. Five Sidhe of the Summer Court were piling out of a Humvee, armor ready for war.

Naerine stood at their head, a pair of pistols strapped to her hips as she advanced on the administration building. Three of her companions were armed with assault rifles, and the fourth had a long cylindrical tube strapped to his back.

At a glance, most of the weapons weren't even legal in Australia. Gun safety laws here were stringent, but clearly the Summer Court didn't pay them much heed.

The two police officers standing out front hesitated. They were outnumbered and outgunned by creatures they had never seen before. They climbed back into the squad car and reversed out of the car park, moving out of the line of fire as they observed the chaos unfolding in the school.

"We're too late," Alasdair breathed. "They're here."

Naerine motioned for her minions to fan out behind her.

Alasdair grabbed Janine. "This is going to get a lot worse before it gets better. Is there somewhere you can hide?"

She looked about. "Yes. I can head to the—"

"Don't tell us," Alasdair replied. "If you don't tell us, they can't pry it out of us. Go now and hide until this all blows over."

Janine nodded and ran for the back door of the administration building.

"The police aren't going to take this lying down, are they?" I whispered.

"I dare say they're calling it in right now," Alasdair said. "Perhaps if they're swift, it might be enough to scare the Sidhe into hiding. Aggressions against normals will bring repercussions from the Arcane Congress."

"But they are the Summer Sidhe, right? Not the Red Cap's minions?"

"Yes," Alasdair replied, "but they don't look like they're here for tea and cookies. I'll try to talk my way out of this but there is every chance they're going to blame this on you."

"Me?" My voice trembled. "How could I even know this would happen?"

"No, not that," Alasdair said. "They'll blame you for the killing. That's ice magic in there, and a lot of it. Absent an aggressor from the Winter Court, they're going to suspect the first ice mage they can find. I am a hunter, but you? Well, when Naerine looks at you, she will know exactly what you are. I stalled them in the grove, but they will recognize the truth if they haven't worked it out already."

So that was it. Alasdair, the Old One. All of them knew who I was, or at least *what* I was. They'd all known before I did. I supposed if he knew exactly who my father was, Alasdair might turn me over to the Summer Court himself. I'd never been good at lying, but given everything my mother had told me the night before, I wasn't sure I could trust him with the whole truth. Alasdair's hatred of the Winter Sidhe ran deep. I couldn't be sure how he would react to the truth. I also didn't want to be pinned between two potential enemies: the Summer Court outside and Alasdair in here.

"What do you mean?" I asked, peering at the Summer Sidhe through the front window. The realization that they could be looking for me scared the hell out of me. I didn't want to believe it was true. After all, I'd been living here all my life in the heart of their realm. Why now?

Neutral ground. Alasdair's words echoed those of the Otherworld journal. I'd started dabbling in their realm, and I had forever left neutral ground.

"Don't bother lying to me," he said. "You're awful at it. Don't fret. It's not in your nature. I know you're a scion. I've suspected it since the moment I met you in the library. I've left it alone because you never gave me a reason to doubt you. Don't start now."

"What do you want me to say?" I asked, confused. If he knew, why hadn't he said anything?

As he looked at me, I could feel his power building.

"Did you have anything to do with this?" He pointed toward the principal's office.

I shook with both fear and indignation.

"No, and how could you even think that?" I replied, hurt.

"Clearly you know more than you're letting on. You were able to get that pixie out of here with no struggle at all. The Old One said the little creature was quite content to follow you. Almost like Winter recognizing one of its own."

The words were harsh, accusatory, and made my blood boil. I could feel the heat rising in my face, my anger growing by the moment.

"How dare you?" I replied. "I didn't even know what I was until last night. And I wasn't here. I was at home with my mother and children. I certainly didn't have any part in this, and I haven't told you a single lie since the day we met."

"You certainly left out a lot of the truth, though," he said, his eyes boring into mine.

"Not on purpose. I'm still processing it myself."

"Then process quickly, because there are five summer Sidhe out there and the man lying on the table dead in there is one of their agents."

"Agents?"

"Yes, why do you think the school is so focused on the environment? Perfectly manicured gardens, an abundance of trees and greenery. Do you think they just decided to be one with nature, or do you think perhaps that it was the predisposition of the man who ran the place? Arthur Dare has long been a friend of the Summer Court. I just can't work out why he hired us to rid the school of that pixie. It's one of the reasons we never moved on the bounty."

"If he knows the Summer Court, couldn't he just have asked them directly?" I replied.

"A question I would love to ask him if he weren't dead," Alasdair whispered back. "But we need to get out of here."

As if she could hear his whisper, Naerine shouted across the lawn.

"Come on out, Alasdair. Bring your new apprentice with you. We want to have a word with both of you."

"I guess they know your bike," I muttered.

"Well, that makes this a helluva lot more dangerous. If they think for a minute you killed Dare, they'll kill us both and sweep the misunderstanding under the rug later with the Congress."

"They can do that?"

Alasdair shrugged. "That's the problem with supernatural affairs. You have to survive to make an issue out of it. If we're both dead, there is no conflicting testimony for the Congress to consider. Whatever they say tends to stand. The Old One can't intervene, that's for sure. Too much chance someone might recognize what he really is."

"Turns out I'm not the only one who is hiding something," I replied. It cemented my belief that there was more to the Old One than met the eye. Something more lingered beneath those black robes.

"Yes, and somehow you all manage to find your way into my life. Little lost puppies wanting to be adopted, or to get me brutally killed. I should have quit this game years ago."

"Come on out," Naerine shouted. "We're not going to ask you again."

"She's not here," Alasdair called. I might not be able to lie, but Alasdair had no such constraint. "It's just me. I came to check what happened to the principal. Looks like the Red Cap got to him."

My heart hammered in my chest as I lowered myself behind the brickwork beneath the window.

"No need to lie to us, Alasdair. We watched you both go in. Now you can both come out and surrender yourselves voluntarily or we will come in after you. If we do, it will end poorly for you both."

"Five versus two," Alasdair whispered. "I don't like our chances."

I was a minor talent on the best of days. The other half of me was an overweight woman in her forties playing at bounty hunting. What the hell was I doing? As I wallowed in self-pity, Alasdair pointed out the window.

"It's a trap."

I raised my head. They already knew I was here, so there was no point in hiding.

In the car park, beyond the Summer Sidhe, an immense rift was opening. It was like someone had torn a hole in the fabric of reality itself.

The Veil had been opened, and through it, for the first time in my life, I beheld the Otherworld.

The frozen alpine landscape was totally at odds with sunny Queensland but the thing that caught my eye was the dozens of goblins and Winter Sidhe racing toward the portal. Two immense ice trolls followed them.

And they were coming right for us.

Chapter 15

As the creatures burst through the rift from the Otherworld, the ground shook beneath the feet of the lumbering trolls. Each of them was easily as large as the troll we'd faced at the library. The behemoths were surrounded by goblin handlers and their masters.

I recognized the goblins from images in the journal, with their hooked nose and elongated ears. Their bluish-green skin was tinged with gray, and they were carrying an assortment of goads and prods to spur the trolls forward.

Behind them were three winter Sidhe armored in blue Sidhe steel.

Naerine had been so intent on me, she hadn't noticed the presence of the Winter Court until they were charging across the asphalt of the car park.

My heart raced as the forces of Winter bore down on us. I scanned their ranks for the visage of the Red Cap, but it was noticeably absent.

Naerine spun, her pistols already in her hands. She was fast; I had to give her that. Her hands tracked the movement of the smaller goblins goading the trolls. She fired in quick succession. Three of them went down before the goblins had made it more than a few meters across the car park.

The Winter Sidhe raised their submachine guns and returned fire. The first round took Naerine in her guts even as she threw herself out of the way.

The Summer Sidhe holding the long cylindrical launcher pulled it to his shoulder, drew a bead on the first troll, and fired. Flames and smoke plumed from the rear of the weapon as a rocket-propelled grenade crossed the car park, slammed into the ice troll, and detonated, scattering chunks of troll over a wide radius. The Winter Sidhe went to ground, returning fire.

The second ice troll reached the Sidhe carrying the rocket launcher. Before he could load a second projectile, the troll brought down its massive axe and cleaved the Sidhe in half. As the halves parted in a fountain of blood, Alasdair dragged me away from the window.

"This is our chance. Let's go while they're busy with each other."

He grabbed my arm and charged through the admin block in the same direction Janine had gone. Heavy weapons fire filled the air.

We raced through the building, pushed open the back door, and ran down the stairs. Well, Alasdair ran; I huffed and grunted as I took the steps two at a time and tried not to break my ankle. If the Sidhe didn't kill me, the exercise just might.

"Where are we going?"

"Out the back," Alasdair said. "Plenty of brush to get lost in."

"They're over here," a high-pitched voice squeaked.

I raised my head to see a pair of little goblins rounding the corner of the brick administration block.

I drew on my power, channeling as much malice as I could into the spell. I sent a withering hail of icy missiles at the pair. At least that was what I'd intended, but I managed little more than to douse the creatures in a sheet of Winter sleet. They looked at each other and laughed.

Alasdair had no such issues. Fire streamed from both of his outstretched hands like flamethrowers, catching the two goblins as they raised their weapons.

Their mirth cost them their lives as Alasdair's fire scorched flesh from bone.

We ran for all we were worth. Gunfire rang out as we darted between the buildings.

"If your entire plan hinges on us outrunning them," I panted, "we're as good as dead."

"You are assuming I have a plan," Alasdair replied. "This is well outside the realm of what I'd anticipated when I woke up this morning."

"You don't have a plan?" I said, my voice breaking.

"No," he said. "It kind of went out the window the second that lot showed up."

I wasn't sure if my ears were playing tricks on me, but as we moved through the school grounds, there was the sound of scurrying creatures all around us, but they seemed to be hiding just out of sight.

Alasdair reached into his satchel, pulled out a pistol, and handed it to me.

"There is no safety," he began. "It's loaded. If you see one of those creatures, just point and shoot. No hesitation. They certainly won't hesitate to kill you."

I nodded tentatively as I felt the cold steel in my hand. My second day on the job felt like it was going to be my last. I had the distinct feeling that this wasn't how training was supposed to go. Given the choice, I doubted Alasdair would have willingly wandered into a fight between the two rival Sidhe courts.

But you had to drag him into it.

"Nora? Are you listening?" Alasdair whispered, trying to keep our exact location hidden.

I nodded. "I've got it."

"Good."

We raced down a path that ran between two classrooms. A goblin appeared from behind the building on our right. Without hesitation, I raised the pistol and pulled the trigger. The creature was only about five meters away, but the handgun jumped like it was a cannon. The report of the pistol firing echoed between the buildings. It was almost deafening for us, but the goblin went down hard. Whatever ammunition Alasdair had loaded it with, blew out a section of the creature's back.

"Well done." He nodded. "That's my girl."

The compliment brought out an odd mix of feelings. Part of me realized I'd just killed a creature of the Winter Court. But I was so high on the adrenaline, it wasn't really sinking in. Besides, that was likely the nicest thing Alasdair had ever said to me.

He stooped down and picked up the creature's weapon, a squat submachine gun. I'd seen them in the movies. They were the kind used in those drive-by shootings. A Mac-10, if my memory served me right. They were horribly inaccurate, but anything was better than nothing.

Alasdair led the charge through the school grounds. I did my best to keep up, but in spite of that, I was falling behind.

"We have to keep moving," he called over his shoulder.

My legs were tired. The lactic acid buildup made them feel like they were made of Jell-O. I didn't want to go on, but if those creatures knew where my house was, the Red Cap could be there at any moment.

My children were there, and I wasn't. I had to fix that as quickly as possible.

I forced myself onward.

"How exactly do we get out of here without your bike?" I called after him.

"We only need to make it through the scrub to the road," he said. "We can hitchhike or call a ride share. We just need to lose these guys first."

We made our way through the grounds, heading for the back fence. As we broke through the last line of buildings, we stopped dead. More than a dozen goblins and a third troll lumbered across the oval toward us.

"We're surrounded," I shouted. "What do we do now?"

I searched about for another avenue of escape, but more of the goblins made their way toward us from every direction. We were trapped.

Alasdair reached into his satchel and pulled out a small canister.

"What's that?"

"We need cover. It will help."

Alasdair pulled the pin on the small cylindrical grenade and threw it out in front of us. The cylinder skittered across the grass and started spewing a thick viscous gray fog. The smoke grenade obscured us from view. Alasdair reached behind his back and drew out his machete.

"*Sùdair*!" Alasdair called as he swung the machete before him. Flame flickered along the blade as he moved it through the air.

I stepped back, but Alasdair seemed to be flailing at nothing. Or so I thought until the blade caught on something I couldn't quite see. Then like a pulled thread, the very fabric of reality parted before us.

On one side of the tear, we stood at the edge of the local school. On the other, a thick verdant forest stretched as far as the eye could see.

"What the…? What did you do?" I whispered.

He grabbed me by the shoulders.

"No time for questions," he said, shoving me through the tear.

I staggered into the portal, and Alasdair charged in after me. With another word, he sealed it shut. The chaos of the school vanished.

In its place the sounds of the lush forest filled my ears. Birds chirped in the trees overhead as they tried to drown out the humming insects. All about us, the forest stretched in every direction, but a well-trodden dirt path wound through it.

"Where are we?" I asked. "And how did we get here? What was that you did with your sword?"

"We are in Faerie, in a dense jungle running along the fringes of Summer's domain. The goblins will be reluctant to follow us here."

"Faerie?" I gasped. "But that would mean we passed through the Veil. You can do that?"

"I don't like to, but it didn't seem like we had any other choice. With those creatures trying to kill us, we needed out and we needed it in a hurry. This seemed like the best of a few terrible choices."

"But won't someone find us here?"

"Soon enough, if we dawdle," Alasdair replied, "but I have no intention of staying. We just need to get past their perimeter before crossing back into our realm. If we stay here long enough, their sentries will find us."

"How do you know where to go?" I asked, turning to take in the massive trunks of the forest trees around us. "And how do you know when to cross back?"

"I don't for sure." He knelt as he caught his breath. "The Veil doesn't work like a door. And Faerie is nothing like our world. It exists in a state of perpetual change. You might pass through the Veil two days in a row and wind up in completely different places. As far as I can tell, it has a lot to do with your intentions when you part the Veil. I was searching for a safe haven, so it guided us here to Sanctuary. This woodland is anathema to the Winter Court. Titania rules here with an iron fist and all the creatures existing here, do so at her whim and pleasure. We should be safe from our pursuers, but should we encounter other Sidhe, they will recognize what you are. That would go poorly for us both."

"What I need is to get home," I replied, "and the quicker the better."

Alasdair nodded. "Then I suggest we head east and after a kilometer, we slip back through the Veil. We should be much closer to your home."

"Has it ever failed you? Passing through the Veil, you could end up anywhere."

"True, but right now anywhere is better than there. I once traveled through the Veil in Scotland and when I crossed back, I was in Canada. But to be fair, I was three sheets to the wind at the time and my spell work left a great deal to be desired. The Sidhe are much better at it though, and have greater control over their passage between realms."

"Can you teach me how to do it?" I asked as we walked.

He scoffed. "Not a chance."

"And why not?"

The sound of insects buzzing was broken only by the crackling of leaves being crushed under our feet.

After a time, he turned to me. "You seem perfectly capable of getting yourself in enough trouble at home in our realm. I don't think it's wise to set you loose in Faerie unattended. Particularly with so many people searching for you."

I let out a sigh and kept trudging along the path. He was right, but that didn't mean I wanted to give him the satisfaction of admitting it.

"Stick to the path and keep your eyes open. If you think the wildlife in Australia is dangerous, it pales in comparison to this place."

"For someone who is meant to be training me, you seem awfully reluctant to actually teach me anything. Why is that?"

"You mean apart from the fact that you're a scion of the Winter Court?" he asked. "The Winter Court is made up of dark and dangerous creatures full of malice and strife. I have been given plenty of reason to distrust the Winter Court and until I can be certain where your loyalties lie, I'm exercising an abundance of caution."

"You do understand, I've never even seen the Winter Court, right?" I replied. "My mother brought me here to Australia before I was born. I know nothing of their ways and have no allegiance to them. I shot the goblin, didn't I?"

"You did," Alasdair replied, "but you were saving your own skin as much as mine. Sooner or later, you will have a choice to make, but until you do, I won't train the hand that kills me. The Old One might think you're worth training but no creature of Winter is going to fool me again."

"What's that supposed to mean?" I asked.

"It means the last time I took a chance on one of your kind, he ambushed and killed my trainees. All three of them in a single morning."

My mind went back to the Camp and the gold coins mounted on the wall. Three of them had died on the same day, almost a year ago.

"The Red Cap," I whispered.

"He passed through town looking for something. He invited us to meet with him, but he turned on us, killing my trainees. I barely escaped with my life."

"Is that why you are so afraid of him?" I asked.

Alasdair whirled to face me, his machete still in hand. "I'm not afraid of anyone."

I wanted to say, you could have fooled me, but with him still brandishing the big machete, I thought better of it.

I stood there silently eying the point of the blade hovering inches from my face, not willing to say anything else that might set him off.

When I said nothing, he slowly lowered the blade.

"It's not fear to know your limitations. The Red Cap has been doing this for longer than we have both been alive. He's stronger than either of us. Hell, both of us put together. It's not fear, Nora. It's wisdom to understand one's place in the world."

There was a rustle in the trees somewhere overhead. I glanced up, trying to track the movement. Then dry leaves crunched as something slithered across the ground toward us. My eyes dropped from the canopy above, and instead zeroed in on its position.

The largest snake I'd ever seen, easily as thick as I was, barreled through the foliage. As the serpent approached, it picked up speed. It reared up and lunged toward me. Alasdair stepped into its path and brought the machete down, cleaving the creature's head clean off.

The serpent's tongue flickered out of its maw, lapping at the dirt before it went still.

Alasdair towered over it, maroon blood still running off the lowered blade of his machete.

"You're not going to lug that all the way back to the Camp for a bounty, are you?" I asked.

"No." Alasdair laughed as I caught my breath. "Creatures killed in Faerie don't count. Only those that wander into our realm."

As he spoke, I caught the rustle again as something moved through the trees above us once more. As Alasdair cleaned his blade, another serpent just as big as the first plunged down out of the canopy. Its jaws were open wide, showing fangs larger than my fingers, poised to deliver its lethal venom.

"Alasdair!"

The creature dove toward his neck. Alasdair turned, but the snake was already almost on top of him.

Somewhere within my mind, I heard the word.

"*Sleá oighir!*" I shouted.

A shard of ice formed of magic burst from my outstretched hand like a spear, racing toward the descending snake. The snake tried for Alasdair's neck, but the spear caught it in its open maw, plunged through the top of its mouth, and impaled its brain. The snake fell out of the tree, landing on the forest floor with an immense thud.

The spear of ice that I'd manifested was lodged in its skull.

I'd done that. *Me*. With a word. Well two, actually. I'd never managed anything like it.

A thrill ran through me, a giddy elation at my victory.

"What are those things?" I whispered, still reveling in my victory.

"The natives," Alasdair replied, staring down at the dead serpent. "We'd best get out of here before more of them show up. Or worse yet, their masters. We're out of time."

Raising his machete, he chanted and then drew his machete through the air, cleaving a gap through the Veil.

I didn't need to be told again. I plunged through the portal, and we emerged behind a large skip bin resting beside a concrete tilt-slab building. Alasdair was right behind me.

I tried to get my bearings and found the glowing neon sign of the 7-Eleven. We were at the gas station a street from home. We had traveled less than a kilometer in Faerie yet here in the mortal realm, we'd covered ten.

It wasn't the U.K. to Canada on a drunken jaunt, but it was something.

Alasdair cleaned his blade against a pant leg and sheathed it.

"We're close, Alasdair," I shouted as I started running. "I need to get home before they do."

Alasdair matched my stride, and we reached the end of my street in record time. Half a dozen of my neighbors were gathered in their front yards staring at something. I followed their gaze to a plume of smoke rising from a house.

My house.

It felt like lead settled in my gut.

Oh, please, no.

I ran. My heart pounded in my chest. I was tired, weary, beaten, but all I could think of were Conor and Shay, my mother, and Sleet.

Everything dear to me in the world was in that house. I ran down the footpath, ignoring my neighbors.

Smoke rose in a choking plume from the rooftop of my home and the front door had been kicked in.

I couldn't bear to think about what lay within.

"Oh no. Please, don't let me be too late," I pleaded to any being that was listening. I bounded up the front steps. "Please let me be on time."

Chapter 16

It was as if a cyclone had gone through my home. Photo frames had been torn off the walls, the glass from their frames shattered across the tiles.

At the entrance to the living room, I found myself stepping over the body of a Winter Sidhe. His smooth features were now still. A cavernous wound in his chest was the obvious cause, and his insides now liberally coated the wall behind him. That was going to cost me my security deposit.

The metallic scent of blood lingered in the air as I stepped over the corpse.

"Mum, Conor, Shay!" I called, hoping someone would answer me. The house was eerily quiet and devoid of the rambunctious noise that so often filled it.

My heart beat faster as I ran to the kitchen and found the source of the smoke. A pot of pasta on the stove had boiled dry and was billowing profusely. I turned it off on the way past and flicked on the exhaust fan. Anything to stop the neighbors calling the fire department, if they hadn't already.

I wasn't sure what I'd say to the police and right now I didn't care.

The door leading in from the back patio had been blasted in, adding yet more glass to the floor. I raced upstairs, calling my children's names again.

When no one answered, I ran into Shay's room. "It's me, baby. If you're here, please say something."

I checked the cupboards, underneath the bed, and behind the curtains. When I found nothing, I headed to Conor's room.

His computer table was overturned, the monitor broken in half on the floor. Several pieces of his art were missing. Others were crumpled on the floor and in amongst them were his noise-canceling headphones. I picked them up and clutched them to my chest. There was no chance Conor would have left them behind voluntarily.

Footsteps behind me warned me of Alasdair's approach. I'd recognize those heavy boots anywhere.

"They're gone," I said, my voice little more than a whisper. I was afraid if I opened my mouth any more, I would cry. "They took them. They took my family."

I expected Alasdair to say he'd told me so. Perhaps he would add something about me being too stubborn and ignoring the many warnings he'd spent days giving me.

Instead, he simply put an arm around my shoulders.

"We'll get them back, Nora, don't worry. We'll get them back."

I shook my head as the yawning pit of despair swallowed me whole.

"He has them. The Red Cap," I sputtered. "My mother, my children, all of them."

I clutched my son's headphones and thought about how terrified he must be. I thought of Principal Dare's tortured body, and tears streamed down my cheeks. I should have been here to protect them. They shouldn't be paying for my mistakes.

"Don't cry, Nora," Alasdair said. "It won't do you or them any good. You'll need a clear head if we're to go after them."

"How?" I whispered. "We haven't so much as laid eyes on the Red Cap. We have no idea where he is, or where they're going."

As if in answer to my question, a loud crisp bark cut off my chain of thought. Then another. The sound grew in volume until the barks were deafening. Each bark shook the glass in the window frames.

I raced to the window. The bodies of three more mauled Sidhe were strewn across the backyard. None of them were moving.

Another bark shook the house.

"What's the...?" Alasdair looked to the window.

"Bran!" I charged out of Conor's room and down the stairs, almost slipping in the process. As my shoes hit the tiles downstairs, another bark rolled through the house. There was something different about the barking; it wasn't his usual good-natured playful rumble. It was loud, abrasive, and full-bodied.

A tingle ran down my spine. It was almost as if there was power in the sound.

Was that even possible? I rounded the corner and there standing amid the glass-strewn tiles was Bran. His mouth was open, his tongue lolling from side to side. The white and gray fur around his mouth was stained red with what I was pretty sure was blood, none of it his.

"Nora!" a high-pitched voice called. It took me a moment to spot Sleet, sitting astride Bran, one hand clinging to his collar as he held on for dear life. "The master, he was here."

I ran over to my dog and hugged him tight. As I looked over his shoulder, the carnage in the back yard became apparent. The mauled remains of three goblins lay where they'd fallen.

"Nora, the master!" Sleet's voice rose higher.

"I know, Sleet. Did you see where he went?"

Sleet shook his head. "Bran and Sleet fought his goblins. When they were all dead, the Red Cap was gone. Sleet tried to find them, but he uses magic to hide."

"Is that a King's Hound?" Alasdair's booming voice filled the kitchen.

"What's a King's Hound?" I asked, as I checked my dog for wounds. Fortunately, he'd given far better than he'd gotten.

Alasdair looked at me, confusion etched on his face.

"This is Bran. He's an Irish Wolfhound. We've had him for years."

"No," Alasdair replied, "that's a King's Hound. They are the chosen hunting companions of the Winter King, bred in his halls from an ancient wolfhound bloodline. They are as much a creature of magic as anything in Faerie. You've had one all this time?"

I didn't want to admit that I had no idea what he was talking about. In light of what I'd learned about my own heritage, it only made me feel foolish.

All I knew was that we had taken Bran in as a stray, or so I'd thought. Given the conversation I'd had with my mother and the knowledge of who my father was, there was a part of me that wondered if Bran hadn't found us.

Alasdair took the headphones out of my hands.

"What are you doing?"

"Finding your son," he replied, bending down in front of Bran. "Glamours won't hide him from a king's hound. They're used to hunting Fae."

Bran bared his teeth, issuing a warning growl, but Alasdair held out the headphones.

"I'm not here to hurt you, boy; behave," he commanded. "They took the children. Can you find them?"

Bran had always responded intelligently to my directions. I always figured he'd just been well trained, but Alasdair spoke as if the big shaggy dog could understand his every word.

Bran regarded Alasdair, then lowered his nose to Conor's headphones. He sniffed at them, raised his nose, and sniffed again.

He gave a single decisive bark and headed for the front door.

"I'll take that as a yes," Alasdair replied. "Let's go. The longer we wait, the greater the chance they have to prepare. If he is after you, it will be a trap."

"I know," I replied. "He's after me, but I can't leave them with him. After what he did to Dare, I won't leave them with him a moment longer than I must."

Alasdair nodded. "The sooner we spring the trap, the better chance we have of living through it."

I raced upstairs, grabbed a heavy coat, and slid the pistol Alasdair had given me into one pocket. In the cupboard I located a box of my ex's things and found a small knife Judas used to gut fish, and slipped its sheath into the other pocket. I wished I had something impressive like Alasdair's machete, but this would have to do.

Downstairs, Alasdair was reloading the weapon he'd stolen from the goblins at the school with ammunition he'd lifted off the dead creatures around the house. Once it was locked and loaded, he tucked the weapon back in his satchel.

"Let's go get my family back," I said, sliding my hand into my pocket and taking comfort from the cold steel I found there.

"If we find them," Alasdair replied, "don't hesitate. Shoot first, ask questions later. The Red Cap won't wait for you."

Clearly, he'd spoken to the Old One. I'd been unwilling to kill Sleet, but that was different. The Red Cap had taken my family. Alasdair had no idea what I was capable of.

"Let's go, boy," I called to Bran and strode out the front door.

"Are you coming or staying?" I called over my shoulder to Alasdair.

If my neighbors thought anything of the pixie riding the blood-soaked hound, they kept it to themselves. A rare exhibition of common sense on their part.

"Fire's out, nothing to worry about," I shouted at Mrs. Grobinsky. "Spread the word."

She looked at me, her jaw hanging open. I was sure I looked a real sight, covered in blood from the creatures we'd killed to get here. My neighbors shuffled back, letting us pass.

"They'll have gone to ground, somewhere nearby," Alasdair told me. "The Red Cap will want to secure his prizes while he sets a trap for you."

"How do you know they haven't fled to the Otherworld?"

Alasdair pointed to Bran who strode down the footpath, sniffing as he went.

"If they did, he'd lose the scent. As long as he has it, they're still here."

I tried not to let panic consume me. Right now, I had everything to lose. My children's lives hung in the balance. As we walked, I tried to distract myself with thoughts of all the things I would do to the Red Cap when I finally got my hands on him.

The Sidhe had taken my whole family, everything in the world that meant anything at all to me. Why? Because I'd liberated a pixie from the Red Cap's employ? My gut told me this was something more. The Red Cap had been hunting here long before I'd met Sleet.

I tried to put together the pieces of the puzzle: the Red Cap's visit to the school, Sleet's escape. The Red Cap's return and subsequent torture of Principal Dare. The more I thought about it, the more convinced I was he'd found exactly what he was looking for.

My family seemed inextricably linked to the Otherworld. The troll finding me at the library, whatever was happening with Conor and his sight.

Was that why the Red Cap was here? Was the Winter King aware of my boy?

Was this all part of some plan to drag us back kicking and screaming to his hall? Would my mother's escape be in vain after all?

Too many questions, not enough answers. It was the story of my life all over again.

Halfway down the boulevard, we reached a nature reserve. It started at a narrow point at the roadside, but broadened in an ever-widening wedge shape covered in dense woodlands. Bran left the footpath and made straight for the reserve.

"They're in there, aren't they, boy?" I whispered.

Bran growled as he prowled through the unmowed grass like a hunting cat. The reserve boasted a multitude of places to hide.

"Careful, Nora, we both know it's a trap."

"I know, but I can't very well leave them with him, can I?"

"No, we can't," Alasdair said, "but we need a plan."

I looked at him. "I thought that was your job."

"Normally, yes. But they are your children. I'll follow your lead. I'll not give the order that gets them killed."

The weight of that responsibility settled heavily on my shoulders, and the voice of my inner critic hastened to spread doubt. I set her aside.

"We spread out," I whispered. "There's too much ground to cover. Besides, if one of us wanders into a trap, it leaves the rest of us the chance to rescue them. If we move together, there is a chance we'll all get jumped together."

"Be that as it may, we shouldn't go far," he said. "Seconds make all the difference in a fight. We need to be close enough to assist each other."

I bent down and whispered to Bran, "You two stay together. Look for the children. If you find them, send word with Sleet. If I call, you come. Got it?"

Bran ducked his head as if to say he understood.

"We'll find them," Sleet reassured me before the pair stalked off into the brush.

We moved into the woodlands. I wasn't much of an outdoorsman, but studying the ground before me, I noted the fallen branches and dried leaves, all of which threatened to give me away. I picked my way through a path, favoring stealth over speed. Alasdair split off to my left, steadily moving away from me.

A blood-curdling shriek split the air.

The cry sent a chill right through me.

My mother's voice groaned. "Do what you will, you pointy-eared bastard. If I get out of here, you're as good as dead."

Some days, my mother seemed like she was made more of concrete and rebar than flesh and blood.

I crept through the forest until I almost stumbled into a clearing.

Three goblins sat in the shade of a cluster of moss-covered boulders. Before them a fire crackled. A rabbit on a spit turned slowly over the flame.

I bit my lip to stop the gasp that threatened to give me away.

At the edge of the clearing, my mother was chained to a tree, her arms suspended against a pair of low hanging branches. Another chain held her ankles together. Blood ran down her face from a wound on her forehead, and pooled beneath her right hand. More of it ran from a dozen small cuts on her arm. Before her, the leering form of the Red Cap gloated over her.

He stood head and shoulders above his fellow goblins, his pasty green and gray complexion spotted with black warts. He was well-muscled and covered in an assortment of the blue steel favored by the Sidhe, worn over the top of a chainmail shirt. On his head he wore a battered red baseball cap, and he boasted a mouthful of teeth that seemed to have been sharpened to a fine point.

My heart skipped a beat. Conor and Shay had been chained together, forced to watch the horrors the Red Cap had been inflicting upon their grandmother. Shay had her eyes closed, tears running down her cheeks. Conor stared on, his teeth gritted, seemingly unable to look away.

"Leave her alone," he shouted.

The Red Cap ignored his entreaty and drew another narrow cut in my mother's arm with the dagger he was holding.

From where I stood, I saw him in profile. I'd only get one shot at surprising him. I needed to make it count. I started circling the clearing.

"All those years lording yourself over the rest of the court," he said to my mother, "all because Oberon thought you were a good lay. Foolish human. You crossed the king and now there is no one left to protect you."

My mother huffed and heaved as she gathered her breath. "You always were a miserable wretch, Desoulis. Good to see nothing has changed. Still a lick-spittle for your betters. It must hurt to be this close to that much power and still have none of it. He could end you with a thought."

The Red Cap leaned in, pressing his dagger against her throat.

"I could end you with a flick of my wrist, and he would never be the wiser. The Winter King's eye is elsewhere, leaving the rest of us free to do as we will. You have no idea what you've set in motion."

"Do it then," my mother hissed. When the Red cap didn't move, she laughed. "Even now, you don't have the stones. Worried you might have overstepped?"

"You're no good to me if you're dead, woman. Don't pretend to know me."

"I know we're more valuable to you alive."

"Not all of you." The Red Cap smirked. "Look at you. Time has not been kind to you, Cara Byrne. The Winter King has no need of a haggard old woman."

If that was true, he could kill her at any moment. I reached into my bag and drew out Alasdair's pistol. No doubt it would be sufficient to signal Alasdair and Bran. Hopefully it would be enough to put a convincing hole in the Red Cap and his plans. A little lead poisoning was just what the doctor ordered.

I stalked around the camp until I had a clear line of fire.

"Don't worry, Cara, you'll get your wish soon enough. There will be no glorious return to the Winter Court for you. Only one of you will live to set foot in Faerie. I just want you to die with the knowledge that your duplicity made all of this possible. If only you'd stayed in *Caisleán Geimhreadh*, none of this would have occurred. Under the watchful eye of Oberon, you would all have been safe."

"Rubbish," she said. "No one is safe there. All live and die at his will."

"The bargaining power of a scion would have brought you status," the Red Cap said, "but you had to run."

Inching forward, I raised the pistol. A twig snapped beneath my boot.

The Red Cap lifted his head, his beady yellow eyes finding me.

I pulled the trigger three times in rapid succession.

The first shot went right past him, striking a tree somewhere in the distance. The second round punched into his left shoulder. The Red Cap hissed in pain, blood oozing from the wound. The third shot went high as I struggled against the pistol's recoil.

"Ambush!" the Red Cap bellowed.

His goblin minions scrambled away from the fire, diving for their weapons.

That was when the moss-covered mound beside them began to move.

The mound rose out of the mud it had been laying in, shaking forest debris from its slumbering form. A sinuous scaly serpentine neck uncoiled as it opened its green eyes, each split with a single vertical slit. The creature stretched its wings and beat them once, sending a breeze through the clearing. The stinger on its tail whipped about, ready to impale anyone foolish enough to get in its way.

The Red Cap had brought a bloody wyvern.

Chapter 17

The Red Cap bellowed in a guttural language I couldn't understand, but from the tone, I got the gist of his meaning.

His goblin minions scrambled toward me, armed with an array of unpleasant implements of death they had scavenged from who knew where. One of them carried a wicked-looking cattle prod, another a crossbow and the third, the most bizarre, a flintlock pistol.

The crossbow-wielding goblin fired as I threw myself behind a fallen log. The steel bolt thunked into the log. He stopped to reload while his companions bore down on me. Worried as I might be about the little murderers, it was the monstrous wyvern, easily four meters tall, stomping through the clearing toward me, that worried me most.

That and the fact the Red Cap had vanished, seemingly into thin air. The cattle-prod-wielding goblin reached the fallen tree and placed a hand on it to vault over it. He was met with a lance of fire as wide as my hand that punched straight through his chest. The creature's eyes bulged as the cattle prod fell from his grasp. It landed in the mud, joined a moment later by the goblin.

Alasdair burst out of the scrub to my left, hurling a ball of fire at the wyvern. The broiling flames struck the creature in the neck, washing over its scales. The beast shook off the attack like a dog wringing water from its fur and lumbered on.

Drawing his machete, Alasdair set the blade alight and charged the wyvern, pulling its attention away from me. The wyvern looked from me to Alasdair and charged after him.

I turned my attention back to the goblins in time to see the flintlock pistol being leveled at me. Without hesitation, I raised my pistol and pulled the trigger. The creature was less than five meters away. Alasdair's hand cannon blew a gaping hole through the critter's torso.

The flintlock pistol discharged, its payload careening wildly into the forest. I leapt over the fallen trunk with a grace that frankly surprised me, and raced toward the third goblin. He was hastily trying to reload his crossbow, but I had no intention of giving him that much time. Huffing and panting, I crossed the space between us and crash-tackled the goblin into the mud.

"Mum," Conor called from the middle of the camp. His chains clinked together as he stood up. Shay echoed his cry.

I turned to them, my babies, chained and shaking in the heart of the unfolding chaos.

"Get down!" I shouted, not wanting a stray projectile to hit them in the chaos that was rapidly consuming the clearing.

The goblin with the crossbow grabbed my arm and plunged his teeth into my flesh, drawing blood.

"Why, you little..." I grunted as I grabbed him by the neck with my free hand and slammed him into the mud. The goblin bared his yellow teeth at me, but I was on top of him. If there was ever a time in my life where I gave thanks for the extra weight I was carrying, it was now. Try as he might, he couldn't buck me off.

He reached for a rusty blade on his belt but I pinned him down, my good hand tightening around his throat. It was him or me, and there was no way I was leaving my children in the hands of these monsters. The image of my mother hanging from the tree burned in my mind as I strangled the life out of him.

The goblin went limp, and I sucked in a deep breath.

Rising to my feet, I searched for the Red Cap.

"Nora, look out," my mother called.

I turned in time for a piece of ice the size of a basketball to slam into my left shoulder, sending me stumbling across the clearing.

A second followed right behind it, slamming into my chest and winding me. I tried to find my breath as I searched in vain for the threat.

The clearing filled with the Red Cap's haunting laughter.

"The scion that would be a hunter. You're a contradiction, Nora Byrne. You never stood a chance."

"Shut up!" I dragged myself out of the mud and to my knees.

"If your father could see you now, he would be ashamed. Hunting your own kind for money. Your death will be everything you deserve."

The hairs on my neck stood on end as he gathered power for another attack. I could feel his presence, but I couldn't work out where he was.

I managed to get to my feet as a hail of icy slivers the size of sewing pins hurtled at me. The tiny shards of ice glinted as they raced toward me. I raised my hands to shield my face and was rewarded with dozens of the stinging missiles piercing my flesh. As the fusillade ceased, I looked down, expecting blood but found my hands turning blue instead.

What are you doing, Nora? You're deluded thinking you could face him.

"Shut up," I bellowed. I wasn't deluded. I was desperate, and fighting not only for my own life, but for my family. I was many things—forty-two, out of shape—but I'd be damned if I'd let cowardice be one of those things.

"Make me." The Red Cap gloated as Alasdair and the wyvern dueled at the edge of the clearing. "You'll die here; your master too. But I'm going to take my time and savor your suffering. It's no less than you deserve for turning against your own. And Cara will watch it all."

"Kick his ass, Nora," my mother shouted, hanging heavily against her chains.

Was it just me or was she paler than before? It had to be the blood loss.

Another icy barrage materialized and rocketed toward me. I dodged beneath it, and it disappeared into the trees behind me.

An ear-splitting bark tore through the clearing as Bran charged out of the foliage. On his back, Sleet still clung to his collar, his little razor blade held aloft as he shouted and whooped his own war cry.

Bran loped across the clearing, snapping at something I couldn't see. The Red Cap howled in pain and reappeared as he lost control of the glamour he'd been hiding behind.

"That's a good boy," I shouted as Bran did his best to tear out the Red Cap's hamstrings.

Sleet launched himself at his former master, wings beating furiously as he slashed at the Red Cap's neck, scoring a glancing blow.

The Red Cap raised his hand and bellowed. Ice gathered around Sleet, as if forming from moisture in the air itself until my little pixie was encased in an ice cube the size of a bucket. Sleet crashed to the ground, his face frozen in a muted scream. The Red Cap kicked the block, sending it skidding across the clearing.

"Foolish traitor, I'll deal with you later."

Bran was not so easily deterred. As the Red Cap tried to ensnare him in an icy prison, Bran thrashed and kicked, shattering the ice even as it tried to form around him.

Racing toward the Red Cap, I reached into my pocket and found the filleting knife. It felt flimsy as I charged a creature who wielded magic with deadly ease.

The Red Cap drew his own knife, a wickedly curved blade tinged with blue, and lunged at Bran. The hound darted aside, the blade passing mere millimeters over his shaggy back.

"Run, boy! Help Alasdair," I shouted as the wyvern towered over my mentor.

Bran barked his acknowledgment. Judas had been an avid rugby fan, and I'd watched enough games to know the virtue of dropping my shoulder.

I slammed into Red Cap.

We both went down, grappling as we fell. I lost my knife but fought him for his.

Unfortunately, he was so much stronger than me. As my grip faltered, I kicked hard against the ground, launching forward and driving my head straight into his chin. His lip burst and the knife dropped into the mud. Drawing back, I gave him the best right hook I could manage. He turned, and my blow glanced off his granite cheek. He laughed as he punched me in the stomach.

I was fighting for my life, and he was enjoying it. As he shifted his weight, I lost balance and he rolled, throwing me off him. Quick as lightning, he was on top of me, pinning my hands to the ground.

I fought him every inch, but he pressed my hands into the mud and with a word, icy manacles froze around them, holding me fast. I kicked, bucking against him to throw him off me, but my ankles were encased in ice manacles of their own. The Red Cap grabbed me by the hair and forced my head to face Alasdair.

Alasdair barely got out of the way each time the wyvern's stinging tail thundered down into the mud with enough force to break bone.

"This is my favorite part," the Red Cap whispered, his black tongue almost brushing my ear. "The slow but inevitable surrender. His death is already assured."

Bran snapped at the creature but the thick armor on the apex predator's flank seemed proof against his teeth.

I tried to turn away, but the Red Cap forced my head back to the ground.

"Look," he hissed. "You will be the death of them. Just as your mother was the death of you."

"I'll kill you, Desoulis." Chains rattled behind me as my mother screamed. "You touch one hair on her head, and I will cut you from groin to gullet, so help me God."

The Red Cap inclined his head toward her and laughed. "No, you won't, Cara. You will watch her die, and then you will join her. This will be your legacy. Only one of them is even fit for the Winter Court."

Conor. He was talking about Conor. I kicked and thrashed but the ice held me firm. The Red Cap raised his hand above me, and a blade of crystalline ice formed in his hand. It was almost a foot long, with a keen edge.

"Any last words, Nora?"

I didn't want to give him the satisfaction, so I willed as much power as I could manage into my hands and legs, trying to break the icy bonds there. Instead, I found myself wrestling with the Red Cap's iron will as he fought to maintain their icy grip.

"Fight him, Nora. You can do it," my mother shouted.

I wanted to, but I simply didn't have the power. He was a creature of Winter, a being of ice and snow. I was only half-Sidhe, and not my better half. I was a minor talent wrestling against a veteran.

I didn't stand a chance.

He raised the blade over my heart. I watched the arm descend.

"Stop!" a shrill voice called.

The Red Cap stopped dead. His hand quivered, but the blade didn't move a millimeter. The veins in his neck bulged as he exerted himself against an unseen power that held him in check.

Conor stood, his hands bound together in chains, his eyes glowing blue as waves of power emanated from him.

"Now, Nora," my mother cried.

"I can't," I shouted back.

Even though the Red Cap was frozen in place, his will still held me in check.

"Look at your boy. That same power is in you," she shouted, her voice on the verge of breaking. "You are so much more than you believe. Put aside your doubts and find yourself."

The Red Cap's lips twitched as he growled something in his own tongue, a series of clicks and whistles. At first, I was worried that it was a spell. Then the wyvern leapt into the air, flapped its wings twice, and slammed into the ground beside Conor, knocking him down. My boy's head struck the ground.

Conor went still, and his hold on the Red Cap broke.

Rage boiled within me like steam with nowhere to go.

The knife descended. My inner critic promised me a swift death. My mother shouted at me to live.

Then within me, I felt something burst, a dam behind which the waters of a mighty river had been held in check but now would no longer be contained.

It broke with a fury that drowned out all the other voices there. It screamed a truth I'd never dared believe. I was no failure, no party trick or minor talent.

It bellowed that I was Nora Byrne, Scion of the Winter Court, Daughter of Oberon the King of Ice and Darkness. Power surged through me like a river until it filled my entire being, yet instead of being consumed by it, I felt comforted.

I willed everything I had at the Red Cap. "*Briseadh*!"

The crystalline blade of the knife exploded, the ice shattering into a thousand shards, as did the icy chains binding me. The Red Cap shrieked as the barrage bracketed his frame.

With my hand free, I pointed it at his chest and bellowed, "*Sleá oighir!*"

A spear of ice formed from my outstretched hand. It drove through the Red Cap's armor, impaling him on a shaft of ice two feet long. The Red Cap coughed and spluttered blood as he keeled onto his side, grasping at the shaft lodged in his chest.

Rising to my feet, I found his knife, the bluish-tinged steel of its haft sticking out of the mud.

The wyvern loomed over my children, ready to strike.

"Don't you dare," I shouted as I made my way back to its master. Knocking the dirty red baseball cap off his head, I grabbed a fistful of his hair and yanked his head back so the wyvern could see the terror in his eyes. I imagined it was a new experience for them both.

I knew what I needed to do. It was the way of things. The way of the hunters demanded it.

"Look away, children," I warned, trying to block their view as best I could.

"I'll kill you for this. No—"

I didn't let him finish the sentence. Bringing his own blade down, I carved through sinew and bone as if they were nothing. His body sank into the mud, and I raised the Red Cap's severed head. The wyvern took one look at its master and launched into the sky, its wings beating furiously as it climbed toward the setting sun.

As the clearing went still and quiet once more, Shay looked up at me, the severed head of the Red Cap still in my hands. They shouldn't have had to see this. Conor was unconscious, which I took to be a blessing. Casting the head aside, I ran to my mother, who was sagging against her chains.

"I'm sorry," she whispered.

"For what? This isn't your fault."

"For everything," she said.

I hugged her tight against me as I fought back tears. I needed to break her out of these chains, but for the moment I was just glad we were all alive.

Bran nuzzled up against Alasdair, who was checking on the children. Conor's little chest was rising and falling. At least he was still breathing.

"You've got nothing to be sorry for," I replied.

Alasdair turned to Sleet who was still encased in the melting ice block. With an effort of will, I accelerated the process, until the pixie was free. He coughed and spluttered as he tested his wings.

"Nora Byrne, we need to talk."

The familiar voice echoed through the clearing.

Turning, I found Naerine, ambassador of the Summer Court, standing there. With one hand she was attempting to staunch the wound in her chest. With the other, she held a silver pistol, leveled right at my face.

She regarded me with unveiled contempt. "Tell me why I shouldn't kill you right now?"

Chapter 18

I stared down the barrel of Naerine's pistol and exhaled.
"You've got to be kidding me," I muttered.
Naerine looked like the walking dead, and her hand shook beneath the weight of her own gun.
Clearly a round she'd taken at the school had found its mark. She was pale from blood loss, and I suspected she was struggling to stay on her feet, a fact which made her all the more dangerous. It didn't take a whole lot of effort to pull a trigger, and she had little to lose.
"To start with, I am not your enemy, never have been. These were." I pointed to the bodies of the Winter Court fae scattered around the clearing.
"I see little difference, other than the fact they are already dead, and you are yet to join them. You are of Winter." Naerine groaned, brandishing the pistol. "I can feel it."
It wasn't much of an achievement on her part. I could feel Winter's might surging through me like adrenaline, perhaps the aftereffects of unleashing it against the Red Cap.
I should have felt relief at the Red Cap's death, and there was certainly some of that. But there was also a part of me that delighted in the gruesome manner of his death. Perhaps that was Winter's influence too. Or maybe it was just me. Too many years spent keeping everything tamped down.

"Most people start with a thank you," I replied, "and beside the fact that I just did your job for you, you are also horrifically outnumbered."

Bran barked as he circled the Summer Sidhe.

"But most importantly," Alasdair added in his Scottish brogue, "Nora is a blooded member of the Camp. Having taken her first bounty, she's one of us. No matter what her genealogy might be, if you lift a hand against the Old One's newest hunter, you can expect to answer to him."

Naerine tightened her hand around her pistol, her knuckles turning white.

"I don't think I'll be answering for much," she replied. "How can I walk away when I know what she is?"

I stared down the business end of the pistol. She had me dead to rights. Before a spell left my lips, I'd catch a bullet for my efforts.

"You might think that," I said, "but I have no issue with you, nor your court, Naerine—unless you make one. This shot is all you have and there's no guarantee you'll even get me."

I was bluffing hard, but there was a truth to it. If she left Conor and Shay orphans, she'd only engender hostilities toward her own kind.

"Look at you," I said. "You're pale, bleeding out, ready to die in the hopes you take one more Winter Sidhe with you. I hate to disappoint you, but I'm only halfsies. So, not really worth it if you think about it. Why not live to fight another day?"

Naerine trembled as she met my stare. She seemed to be clinging to consciousness by raw willpower.

"Naerine," Alasdair said, "you stubborn sun-loving doolally, if you won't think of yourself, think of the consequences."

"Consequences?" Naerine repeated.

"Yes," Alasdair said. "The Summer Court set the Red Cap's bounty, did it not?"

"This has nothing to do with that. This is about what she is. This is about my men that died today trying to drive her kind out of our domain."

"You might think that, Naerine, but how will the Congress feel when we tell them a hunter took a bounty the Summer Court placed and then rather than pay it, you hunted down and killed one of our own?"

"Lies," Naerine spat. "She is one of them. That's why she must die."

"You can believe that all you like," Alasdair said, "but you will be dead and we'll be happy to tell a very different story. If you pull that trigger, you better believe the Congress will hear about it. With no conflicting testimony, that will be the story that stands. And while Summer might be on the rise, you have ground to make up after such a long Winter. You can't afford to fight a war on two fronts. That's how this ends."

Naerine groaned. Relenting, she holstered her pistol.

"This isn't over," she said, her voice raspy.

I looked at the wound in her stomach. "Unless you have someone see to that, soon, I'm afraid it might be. Now lay down and let us have a look at it before you bleed to death."

"Don't you dare touch me," she replied.

Turning her back on me, she raised a finger and parted the Veil as if it were little more than a curtain. Through the rift, the verdant jungle we had passed through earlier came into view.

"Oh, Naerine," I called after her.

"What?" she asked as she limped toward the lands of Summer.

I nudged the Red Cap's head with my foot. "I expect prompt payment for this one. The Old One can tell you where to send the funds."

Naerine didn't even look at me. She simply flipped me the bird.

"Must be some sort of weird Sidhe farewell," I said to Alasdair, loud enough to be sure Naerine couldn't miss it. "Pretty sure it means, peace among worlds."

Alasdair laughed as the Veil closed. It was good to know my mentor had the same taste in TV I did.

Stooping down, I rummaged around the Red Cap's belt until I found a set of keys. I freed my children and my mother. In spite of her injuries, she fought to stand on her own two feet, resisting any effort to carry her.

"I'll be fine. I've had worse," she said. She was bleeding from a split on her forehead and the wounds the Red Cap had inflicted down her arm. "See to the children." I shook my head. She was of good Irish stock. A little blood wasn't going to stop her.

Shay wrapped her arms tight around me, sobbing into my shoulder.

"It's okay. They're gone, baby. None of them will ever hurt you again."

"Unless you count that wyvern," Alasdair chimed in. "I dare say he could do some real harm."

I glared at him. He was doing nothing to reassure my children.

"Not helpful," I growled.

Alasdair raised both hands. "You're right. It's a problem for tomorrow. Let's get you all home."

Bending down, he picked up Conor like he weighed nothing at all and, draping my son over his shoulders, headed for the road.

"What do we do about them?" I asked, pointing at the bodies of the dead goblins.

"They should be fine here for now," Alasdair said. "I'll come back later and take care of them."

I found a burlap sack by the fire, then scooped up the head of the Red Cap, before slinging the bag over my shoulder like Santa Claus from hell.

Together, we made our way home. I hurt all over, but I focused on just putting one foot in front of the other. It was an effort, but I couldn't rest until I saw my family safe.

By the time we reached our street, the crowd from earlier had dispersed, save for the lone figure of Mrs. Grobinsky who was standing on her front lawn, staring at something in my yard.

"What on earth is she up to?" I wondered aloud.

"Mum, isn't that Rex?" Shay asked, pointing to a little fluff-ball squatting on its rear haunches in my yard.

The obnoxious little pooch was busy doing its business in the middle of my lawn.

I drew on my power but received a sharp look of reproach from Alasdair.

"Don't you even dare," he said. "We're better than that."

I groaned as the little puppy commenced a steaming number two. The fact his owner was watching the whole thing only served to elevate my blood pressure.

"Why, I ought to..." I muttered as Rex legged it, leaving his business behind. My frustrations started to well up within me.

No sooner had the idea formed in my mind than I found my lips uttering the command. *"Gaoth!"*

An arcane blast of winter's wind struck the poodle poo with prejudice, sending it flying across the street where it rained down on Mrs. Grobinsky and her beloved patagonias.

A bespeckled Mrs. Grobinsky was still quaking on the kerb, when we reached her.

"I'd appreciate it if you would clean up after Rex in future. You'll note you never find Bran's business on your lawn."

I bent down and ruffled the fur on his head, taking care to avoid the goblin blood staining the fur around his mouth.

"Who's a good boy?"

Mrs. Grobinsky took one look at Bran and hurried for her front door.

"We're meant to protect, not torment, Nora," Alasdair lectured in his thick Scottish accent.

"Whoops, guess I'll have to work on that one," I replied as the old gossip disappeared inside. She reappeared at the window a moment later, glaring at the lot of us.

"I suppose today I'm willing to make an exception," he said with a mischievous grin I found intensely endearing.

I smiled all the way home.

The front door of my house was in ruin, swinging erratically as it dangled from its one remaining good hinge. As we crossed the threshold, I paused.

"Alasdair, do you think you could stay here and watch them? There is one more thing I still need to take care of."

"What's that?" my mother asked.

I held up her burlap sack. "I have to stop by the Camp."

"I can do that." Alasdair smiled, and I sensed a deep satisfaction there. After all, I wasn't the only one who'd had business with the Red Cap. Alasdair had lost three trainees to the murderous Winter Court noble. Today, they'd been avenged.

As I turned to leave, he called after me. "You did well today, Nora."

I tried not to blush, but the praise caught me off guard.

"Thanks," I whispered, feeling like a gawkish girl as I headed out the door. "You all behave. I'll be right back."

"Oh, I'll behave all right," my mother called after me. "Alasdair and I need to talk."

I laughed all the way to the car, not sure if leaving them together was a great decision, but I had no other choice. I wanted to be rid of the Red Cap, and the sooner the better.

The journey to the Camp was the smoothest part of my day. It was as if the usually slow local traffic knew better than to cross me. Perhaps I ought to travel around with severed heads more often.

Parking on the street, I grabbed the sack and headed for the dusty sliding door that served as the Camp's street-front access.

The Old One sat at the kitchen table, veiled as always, slowly stirring a cup of his putrid tasting tea. I knew better now than to ask for my own.

The Old One inclined his head. "What are you doing here? Where's Alasdair?"

"He's watching over my family," I replied. "We ran into a little trouble at the school."

I paused as I considered my words carefully. "Then a little more in Faerie and a hell of a lot of it when I got home."

"Anything I should be concerned about?" the Old One asked, setting down his spoon.

"Well, you're going to need to update the old board over there."

I set the sack on the table, and the blood started seeping through onto the aluminum surface. The Old One leaned forward, running a gloved finger through the blood. Before I could protest, he lifted his finger to the slender gap in his veil where his lips were.

"Mm, Winter." He smacked his lips together. "Goblin, if I'm not mistaken."

"You wondered if I had what it took. I hope this settles your concern. When it matters, I'll do whatever it takes."

The Old One nodded. He opened the sack, reached inside, and drew out the Red Cap's head.

I was expecting surprise, but he calmly rested the head atop the folded sack and leaned back in his chair.

"I'm glad to see my expectations were not misplaced with you, Nora Byrne."

He raised his tea to his lips and took a long sip.

"You knew all along, didn't you?"

"Knew what, dear?"

"You knew what I was," I said, not able to say the words myself.

"Why do you think I greeted you with a knife in the back? Your people and mine are not friends, Nora Byrne, but for you, I'm willing to make an exception. You've answered justice on one who has crossed the Camp. That goes a long way with me, but in time you'll need to reconcile that for yourself."

It dawned on me that I had no idea who or what the Old One was, and as I sat there watching him calmly sip his tea, it gave me pause.

I'd just cut off the Red Cap's head and set it on the table. If my people and his were enemies, he appeared utterly unconcerned with the fact. Which either meant he had the greatest confidence in my goodwill, or he didn't consider me a threat. One of those thoughts was hugely reassuring; the other, utterly terrifying.

I considered asking but thought better of it. He had given me a chance when no other would. He deserved the benefit of the doubt.

Hell, he'd seen something in me that I hadn't even seen in myself until today.

"You'll get nothing but gratitude from me," I replied. "I don't care what our people think of each other."

"You are different," the Old One concluded. "We could use that around here—if you're willing to stay?"

I smiled. "You're not getting rid of me that easily."

"Good," he replied, his lips drawing back into a smile. "I will see to your payment, but we ought to start with this."

He reached inside his robe, drew out something gold, and flicked it to me. With reflexes that surprised myself, I snatched it deftly out of the air.

"A dollar?" I asked. "I think we might be a little short."

"Your payment will come soon enough, but money can't buy you one of those."

I looked down at the coin in my hand and realized it wasn't a one-dollar coin at all. It was larger, and a little thicker and bore on each face a six-pointed snowflake that perfectly filled the surface.

It was a hunter's coin. My coin.

"You're one of us, now, Nora Byrne. What you make of it is up to you."

I held up the coin and smiled. Maybe forty was the new thirty after all.

"We should talk about what comes next." The Old One set down his teacup. "I suspect things are going to grow complicated."

I tucked the coin into my pocket. I wasn't really in the mood for anyone to rain on my parade. "What makes you say that?"

"Well, let us consider the consequences of your actions. Today you killed and cut off the head of a noble of the Winter

Court. Sure, he was trespassing in our realm, but the Winter King cares less for such minor details and everything about his reputation in protecting his vassals."

"He took my children," I replied. "I'll do that and more to anyone who comes for my family."

The Old One held up his gloved hand. "If that wasn't enough, you did it at the behest of the Summer Court."

His words sunk in as I processed what he was saying.

"Today, you are a hunter, Nora; a wealthy one at that. But you must reconcile yourself to the knowledge that what you did today will echo through Faerie, and Winter will answer. He always does."

"Good," I muttered. I wasn't letting anyone kill my mood. I waved as I headed for the door. "Let's hope he stops by soon."

"The foolishness of youth," the Old One whispered as he picked up his tea.

The Old One might know what I was, but I dare say he didn't know exactly who I was. He couldn't fathom just how long I had been waiting for this.

It was time Dad and I had a real heart-to-heart.

The End

Thank You For Being Here

I hope you had a blast with *Bounty Hunter Down Under*. I had a ball writing it and am really excited for the next books in the series: *A Bay Of Angry Fae* & *Ghosts At The Coast*.

If you're new to my books, I'm S.C. Stokes, but most people call me Sam. I'm actually from the town featured in BH Down Under, Beenleigh! I thought it would be fun to set something here.

This was my first Paranormal Women's Fiction and I hope you enjoyed it. When the idea for Nora Byrne came to mind, I thought it was the best genre for her story. Traditionally I write fast-paced urban fantasy, most of which is set in the same universe Nora is from.

So, if you had a ball here, I'd suggest checking out my *Conjuring a Coroner* or *Urban Arcanology* series. You can get the first book free, when you join my newsletter (along with a pile of other goodies and the latest news on my books).

Before you dive into the glossary and the mischief (I mean, linguistic exposé waiting for you there), I just wanted to say thank you for being here.

I'm an indie author, and your support makes all this possible. So thanks for reading *Bounty Hunter Down Under*. If you enjoyed it, spread the word as it helps other readers take a chance on a new series.

If you'd like to leave a review, you can do that here.

Until next time,
S.C. Stokes

P.S. Would you like a free novel to enjoy, you can join my newsletter here, or relax with some other like-minded readers in my Arcanoverse group on Facebook.

Glossary Of Aussie Slang

If you missed the note before the book began, I'd definitely recommend it. I also wanted to be sure to include a full glossary of any Aussie or other slang terms and other choices I made in *Bounty Hunter Down Under*. I hope you enjoy them in the spirit in which they were included. If I've missed something shoot me an email and let me know!

Firies – Firefighters. The only people with the courage to run into a burning building while everyone else is running out of it.

Napisan – Sidhe magic in a plastic tub. It will get stains out of anything. You better believe Mrs. Grobinsky is heading for the Napisan right now.

Petrol Station – Legalized highway robbery. I figured everyone knew this one, but if you ever want to pay five bucks for a loaf of bread, these guys have you covered. Don't even get me started on petrol prices right now.

Bunnings – The only hardware chain in Australia worth visiting. Their helpful staff are exceeded only by the deliciousness of their sausage sizzle. Not sure what's in them, MSG and narcotics probably, and I hope they never stop.

Transport and Main Roads – Our state's equivalent of the DMV. Spoiler alert, you'll never have the right form, and no amount of preparation will get you out of there in less than three hours. To give them their due, they have been improving in recent years.

WD40 – If it squeaks WD40 will stop it, shouldn't be applied to children or rodents.

Roundabout – When an intersection won't do, put in a circle and pray that your neighbors understand right of way. I know other countries have them, but Australia loves roundabouts with a passion Ed Sheeran could write a love ballad about.

Boot – The black hole in the back of your car that gets filled with everything your family has ever used. It gets emptied once in a blue moon but can never be relied on to have what you need. I get it though, 'all that junk inside your boot' is far less compelling (and perhaps far more confusing) as a song lyric.

Thongs – Some passages in *Bounty Hunter Down Under* might be made a little more awkward if you're unaware of the laziest footwear in existence. There is a little Beenleigh slang for when someone forgets one of their thongs, but we've gotta save something for *A Bay of Angry Fae*.

Cuppa – One portion of tea or coffee. Like most Australian slang, we took the word, and made it shorter.

Choc Chip Muffins – I know you don't need a translation here, but nobody's got time for all those syllables, Choc Chip is where it's at.

Kerb – The edge of the road, possibly the most dangerous place to stand in Beenleigh. You think you're safe. That's when they get you.

Skip Bin – A large open top dumpster people get for their front yard so that they can fill it with green waste. How else do you expect them to hide the bodies?

Snags – Are sausages. Nothing smells quite so good as a few snags and onions on a BBQ when you are hungry.

Five Finger Discount – When you take something without paying/asking for it. It's the kind of antisocial activity the boys in blue will pick you up for.

As for the other linguistic choices in *Bounty Hunter Down Under*, I went with US English (in spite of the setting) as that is what most of my readers are used to from me. If this was my first rather than my twenty-first novel I probably would have done differently.

I chose to use 'Mum' in dialogue as that is certainly how you would hear it if you were here. As for measurements of distance, I went with what I would use in the circumstances so those instances are as Australian as I am.

I hope you can forgive these minor inconsistencies in the pursuit of a more flavorful read. Join us for some more fun in *Bay of Angry Fae*.

Have You Read A Date With Death?

When my boss asked me for a favor, I didn't know it was going to get me killed.

As a coroner, discovering the cause of death is literally my job but I'm meant to do it in a morgue, not a mega-mansion. The deceased? Lester Harrington, a reclusive wizard with more wealth than parenting skills.

His five entitled brats have gathered to divide daddy's estate but my autopsy has turned up an unpleasant truth; one of them is a killer that just doesn't want to share.

No job is worth this madness, but unless I can find the killer, my only way out of here is in a body bag.

For your free copy of *A Date With Death,* just tell me where to send it.

About the Author

Sam is a writer of magically-charged fantasy adventures. His passion for action, magic and intrigue spawned his Arcanoverse; a delightfully deluded universe that blends magic, myth, and the modern world in a melting pot that frequently explodes.

When he isn't hiding away in his writing cave, his favorite hobbies include cooking, indulging sugary cravings, gaming, and trying to make his children laugh. You can find more of his work at www.samuelcstokes.com or connect with him at the links below.

a https://www.amazon.com/S-C-Stokes/e/B0161CBT5U

f https://www.facebook.com/SCStokesOfficial

g https://www.goodreads.com/author/show/3043773.S_C_Stokes

BB https://www.bookbub.com/authors/s-c-stokes

ALSO BY S.C. STOKES

Conjuring A Coroner Series

A Date With Death

Dying To Meet You

Life Is For The Living

When Death Knocks

One Foot In The Grave

One Last Breath

Until My Dying Day

A Taste Of Death

A Brush With Death

A Dance With Death

Death Warmed Up

Death Sentence

Urban Arcanology Series

Half-Blood's Hex

Half-Blood's Bargain

Half-Blood's Debt

Half-Blood's Birthright

Half-Blood's Quest

A Kingdom Divided Series

A Coronation Of Kings

When The Gods War

A Kingdom In Chaos

Bones Of The Fallen

A Siege Of Lost Souls

Manufactured by Amazon.ca
Bolton, ON